His self-control went up in flames

Jake pulled her nightgown open, causing the buttons to rip loose like the tides of desire that drove him. Julie reached out to him.

"Don't touch me yet," he said between gritted teeth. "I can't stop if you touch me."

"I don't want you to stop," she almost whimpered, holding him so close that he had trouble drawing in a desperate, ragged breath.

He carried her to the bed, ripping off his shirt. He kicked off his boots, struggled out of his jeans. Julie had already stripped off the torn nightgown and flung it aside.

Their bodies joined with an urgent inevitability, and he held her tightly, saying her name like a prayer as she welcomed him inside her. Feeling her body's answering pulses, he gave himself to her completely, while his blood thundered in his ears like a war drum.

We can't escape this, Julie. We were meant for each other.

Dear Reader,

I can't resist a mystery, and neither can my dynamic hero, vice cop Jake Good Thunder.

Half Irish, half Cheyenne, Jake is as untamed as the criminals he brings down. He loves living on the edge, he thrives on taking risks. He moves easily through the most dangerous of underworlds. He's wily, resourceful, irreverent and has only one weakness—the beautiful Julie Fitzjames.

Jake is an irresistible rebel who, despite his cynicism, has a cause. And it's that integrity that Julie counts on when she has nowhere else to turn. When her aunt vanishes mysteriously, Julie needs the best. And the best is Jake Good Thunder. But she has no intention of succumbing to his charms again. He's broken her heart once before.

Together, Jake and Julie are thrust into a web of mystery, implicit murder and the complicated passions of the human heart. I hope you enjoy this tempestuous pair—and the puzzle that reignites all their former fire…and then some.

Happy Reading,

Lisa Harris

A MAN FROM OKLAHOMA
Lisa Harris

Harlequin Books

TORONTO • NEW YORK • LONDON
AMSTERDAM • PARIS • SYDNEY • HAMBURG
STOCKHOLM • ATHENS • TOKYO • MILAN
MADRID • WARSAW • BUDAPEST • AUCKLAND

ISBN 0-373-25710-4

A MAN FROM OKLAHOMA

Copyright © 1996 by Lisa Harris.

This edition published by arrangement with Harlequin Books S.A.

Printed in U.S.A.

1

SHE WAS DOING what she'd sworn she'd never to do again; she was waiting for Jake Good Thunder.

Julie FitzJames sat in El Rayo Del Sol, the finest Mexican restaurant in Austin, Texas, but the rich, spicy scents of food did not tempt her. Her stomach knotted in anxiety.

It was bad enough Julie had agreed to meet Good Thunder again. Now, as usual, he was late—fifteen minutes late, in fact.

She would never have put herself in this predicament if she hadn't been worried half to death about Rebecca. Yes, she thought, her fears for Rebecca were the only reason she was letting Good Thunder back into her life.

Julie sipped her dark, sweet sangria and studied the masks decorating the wall. Masks—how fitting. They grinned as if to mock her.

All the masks portrayed a smiling sun god, but no two were alike. Some were of clay, some plain, some colored with a rainbow of bright glazes. There were those of wood, gilded metal, pâpier-maché and painted tin. On some, the corona was spiky and geometric; on others, the rays curved sinuously; on a few, they bloomed out gently, like flower petals.

Jake Good Thunder is a man of many masks, she warned herself. *That's why he's dangerous.*

She took another sip of sangria to fortify herself. In the background, a lilting Mexican tune played, its cheerfulness grating on her nerves.

Then, suddenly, although the music was playing, she no longer heard it. From her table, she couldn't see the door, but it didn't matter; the old emotional radar still worked. Jake was there—a deep, fluttery, almost mystical feeling told her so.

Her body tensed and her pulse quickened, just as it had always done when she'd sensed his nearness. Keeping her eyes trained on the stiff smiles of the masks, she tried to make her own face unyielding.

This time she would control her reaction to him or die trying. But then she heard his voice and, despite her resolve, she flinched.

"Julie," he said with lighthearted scorn. "As beautiful as ever. Of course."

The words, the familiar tone, pierced like a blade that cut off her breath. But she tossed her dark hair and looked up, giving him a cool, measured smile. "Jake," she said. "As late as ever. Of course."

For a few charged seconds they simply stared at each other. Slowly he smiled his one-edged smile. *My God*, she thought. *It ought to be illegal to be that good-looking.*

He was six feet three inches tall, with wide shoulders, and a lean waist. His cowboy boots added another two inches to his height. Low-slung jeans, tight and faded, hugged his muscular legs, and he wore a long-sleeved white shirt of western cut, open at the collar. Its snowy whiteness set off the bronze of his skin.

Jake Good Thunder was half-Irish and half-Cheyenne. His Irish blood gave him the to-hell-with-it glint in his dark eyes, the irreverence in his smile and the deep, devilish dimples that creased his cheeks. It had also put the unexpected wave in his thick blue-black hair.

But his face, for all its deceptive charm and amiability, took its strong lines and angles from his Cheyenne father. He had high cheekbones, a beautifully aquiline nose, thin but well-cut lips and a deep cleft in his chin.

In his left hand he carried a white Stetson, and with a pang, she remembered how fine he looked in that hat, its brim at a rakish angle.

He put his right hand on her shoulder and bent toward her. Her heart pounded traitorously hard.

"Late?" he said in his easy, teasing way. "Give me a break, Julie. It stormed in Tulsa. My flight was delayed. Anyway, I'm here. Hello, brown eyes."

Then he leaned closer and kissed her full on the lips. She was helpless to resist. His kiss was brief, but it was no polite peck. It was hungry and tender, sensual and controlled at the same time. It reminded her all too strongly of how he used to kiss her, and the memory shook her to her soul.

"Your mouth tastes like sweet wine," he whispered against her lips. "I wonder if the rest of you still tastes as sweet."

She drew back swiftly, blinking in confusion. "Stop your Irish blarney," she said. "All you're going to taste here is Mexican food."

"Is that right, my little tamale?"

"Sit," she ordered and pointed at the chair opposite hers. "And behave."

He shrugged, and his shoulder muscles did extraordinarily interesting things under the taut fabric of his shirt. She remembered those shoulders bare, hard and powerful beneath her hands, his unclothed body warm against hers. She shook the thought away.

He sat. "You're blushing," he said. "What are you thinking about?"

"Tostadas," she lied. She was relieved when the waiter handed her the large, leather-covered menu. Raising it like a shield, she hid behind it.

She fought hard against the excitement he'd reawakened in her. For two years she'd struggled to forget the sexual spell he'd always cast on her. No other man had ever made her react this way. *Damn*, she thought. *Damn, damn, damn, damn, damn.*

An awkward silence fell between them.

"I caught a cab at the airport," he said at last.

"How resourceful," she said.

"Don't you want to know where my luggage is?" he asked.

She kept the menu between herself and him. She had a will of iron, but she was using all of it to force herself to be the usual Julie FitzJames, calm, rational and independent.

"Why should I wonder about your luggage?" she asked.

"Because I do," he said sarcastically. "They lost it. All I've got is the clothes on my back. If anything happens to these, I'll have to go around naked as a jaybird."

Julie refused to let herself blush again. She remembered him naked, of course. Her artist's eye had found his body truly beautiful; it was long, lean and perfectly muscled.

"We can find you some clothes," she said loftily. "There are stores in Austin. This isn't the moon, you know."

"No," he said, his voice suddenly serious. "When you left to come back here, it seemed farther than the moon. Much farther. You never answered my letters. Did you even read them?"

She took a deep breath, then put down the menu and met his eyes. "Yes," she said. "I did. They didn't leave much room for reply. You like being who you are, doing what you do. And I told you—I can't deal with that."

She turned her gaze away from him and stared again at the masks on the wall. She'd met Jake when she'd gone to Oklahoma City on assignment. She was an artist and illustrator, and a damned good one.

Her specialty was painting flowers, and she'd been hired to go to Oklahoma to do a series of studies on Mrs. David Standish's famed English rose collection. Who would have thought that an innocent garden of roses could lead to so much trouble, so much regret?

SHE'D MET Jake at a party and been immediately smitten. He was intelligent, funny, stunningly handsome and so masculine he radiated a sexuality that made the other men in the room seem like mere phantoms.

He'd been just as taken with her, and people said they made a striking pair. She was tall and willowy, with dark, wavy hair that fell almost to her hips. She had full lips, a slim nose and long-lashed brown eyes; "Bambi-eyes," he used to say, teasing her.

They'd met in June. During the day, she'd studied the roses in Mrs. Standish's formal garden. The Oklahoma sky dazzled her with its blueness, and the perfume of flowers intoxicated her. The colored blossoms ravished her sight: red and white, yellow and peach and orange-gold, the roses bloomed bright amidst their flawless foliage.

She sketched them, photographed them, experimented with watercolor and oil paint. She felt drunk on their beauty all day, then drunk with infatuation for Jake all night.

He was her soul mate, she'd thought. She'd been taken with him on every level, physical, mental, spiritual. She adored his intelligence, his strength and his sense of humor. He seemed to be just as caught up with her.

She'd been so wildly in love that she didn't notice how evasive he was about what he did for a living.

He was taking some time off, he said, to recover from an injury. What kind of injury? Work-related, he'd said, something that had happened on the job. He worked for the state, he said. He'd gotten hit with some metal, an ugly little accident, he reassured her.

He had a fresh white scar on his right thigh, and he was still recovering; he walked with a slight limp. He would go back to work in a few weeks, he told her, and he might be transferred to Tulsa. Julie had felt bereft at the thought of his leaving, then giddy with happiness when he asked her to come with him.

Her assignment for Mrs. Standish was almost done; she'd completed six small preliminary paintings and could do the final work in her studio. Julie's permanent home was a funny little rented house outside of Austin, in the hill country. She loved it and her cramped, makeshift studio, but she would let her lease run out—what did a house matter when she was so much in love?

Jake said they'd find studio space for her in Tulsa. They talked of getting married, and he gave her the engagement ring that had belonged to his Irish grandmother. They settled on a Christmas wedding date.

Those six weeks in Oklahoma City, she and Jake had been deliriously happy, and for the first time in her life, she understood the wild, fulfilling pleasure of sex. Her body and soul were addicted to his, and it felt heavenly.

But then, just as she was getting ready to go with him to Tulsa, she learned what he did for a living. And she felt betrayed, duped, an utter fool.

He was an undercover vice cop for the state police. He was recovering from a gunshot wound that had severed an artery, nearly killing him. Now he intended to go back to undercover work, and she was both frightened and appalled.

He worked on the drug squad, the most dangerous and volatile division of vice, and the more she questioned him, the dirtier and riskier his job seemed. She was shaken to realize how much he loved it. He *liked* living on the edge, gambling with danger.

They'd had their first argument, but it would not be their last. She went to Tulsa with him, and they were lucky enough to find a loft apartment that had a studio room with northern exposure. It had belonged to a painter specializing in western subjects, but his family was growing, and he'd needed a larger place.

It was a wonderful apartment, and Tulsa was a wonderful city. But Julie hated Jake's job, and every day she grew to hate it more.

He slept days, he was gone nights. His shift was supposed to be eight hours long, but often it ran ten or twelve or even sixteen. He told her, in his flippant way, that when he was setting up a suspect for a drug bust, he couldn't exactly punch a time clock.

She came to hate not only the risks he took, but the deception he lived. He moved with perfect ease among the seamiest people in the drug underground. He befriended them, drank with them, won their trust.

In the end he would play traitor, and this didn't seem to bother him in the slightest. She saw it as a sordid charade. He relished it.

Her distaste affected her work, and it affected their relationship. She could hardly sleep at night, and when she did, she had nightmares of him lying hurt and bleeding.

He didn't want to tell her the details of what he did. "The less you know, the better," he would say. When she did wheedle particulars out of him, the truth horrified her, and they'd quarrel again. She wasn't cut out to be a policeman's wife. He would have to realize that. He would have to change.

He tried to quell her fears by bringing home other cops working undercover. "It's just a job," he'd tell her. "And it has to be done." She met these men, but could not comprehend how they so calmly lived their double lives.

Some of them were married, and she met a few of their wives, as well. She found it even harder to understand these women who accepted their husbands' dangerous jobs so blithely. "I don't ask him about it, and he doesn't tell me," one told her with a calm shrug. "It's easier that way."

Of the men he introduced her to, her favorite was Billy Cable. He was only twenty, fresh out of police academy and so baby-faced his fellow officers had nicknamed him Billy the Kid.

Billy was learning undercover work because he'd been given an assignment in the town of Zara. A lot of drugs were floating around among the teenagers of Zara, and Billy was supposed to infiltrate and find the source. It would be his first undercover job.

Jake invited the young vice cop over for an early supper his last night in town, and Billy was alternately proud, nervous and excited. All the talk at supper was cop talk; Billy was full of questions, and Jake was full of war stories.

Julie heard Jake tell tales she'd never heard before, and they chilled her to the marrow. After Billy was gone, they argued again.

"You never told me before that anybody pulled a knife on you," she accused.

"It was no big deal," he said, and she found the statement infuriating.

"Two men held a knife to your throat, and it's no big deal?"

"I told you. I just kept talking. I talked my way out of it. By the end of the night, we were buying each other beers."

"Oh, yes," Julie said angrily. "You talk a wonderful game. *I* certainly fell under your spell. But some day you're going to get yourself in a fix that charm and fast talk won't get you out of."

"I never fast-talked you. I never tried to cast a spell on you."

"Then why didn't you tell me the truth about yourself?"

His lean face went tense. "I waited, that's all. I didn't want to scare you off. I just sidestepped your questions. I didn't lie."

"Maybe you lie so much on the job, you don't even realize when you lie off it. It's become second nature to you," she retorted.

"Julie, I love you," he said, exasperation in his voice. "Do you love me?"

She stared at him for a long moment, her eyes brimming with angry tears. He was Jake—*her* Jake. He looked strong and handsome and unexpectedly stern. "Yes," she said helplessly, and went to his arms. "I love you."

He held her tightly, so tightly that it hurt. "We'll make it work," he said fiercely and kissed her.

They'd made love almost desperately, and during the days that followed, they were careful not to speak of his work again. But Julie was haunted by the feeling that things weren't the same between them.

Then, two weeks later, Billy the Kid was dead, murdered. His body had turned up in a field outside Zara, Oklahoma, a bullet in the back of his head. Julie was shocked, grief-stricken—and angered at the senseless tragedy of it. She and Jake had their final fight.

"You've got to get out of this craziness," she'd pleaded. "Jake, I can't take it. Some day it might be you, and I can't stand thinking about it. You've got to quit. Or I'll go. I swear I will."

The mischievous glint in his eyes was gone, and instead he wore a look that turned her heart to ice. The set of his mouth was bitter and stubborn. "I'm going to Zara. I'm going to find out who killed Billy."

She took off her engagement ring. It was a simple ring with a small stone, old-fashioned and humble, but Julie had loved it. "If you go, I'll leave you," she threatened, and she meant it.

Jake looked her up and down with that foreign coldness in his gaze. "I told you. I'm going. I'll find who did it if it's the last thing I do."

If it's the last thing I do. The words hit her as hard as if he'd struck her. He didn't love her; if he did, he couldn't do this.

She threw the ring at him. It hit him on the cheekbone, but he didn't react at all. The ring fell to the floor and he let it lie there.

"I'm going to West Siloam to see Billy's mother," he said.

Her heart pounded so hard she thought it would choke off her breath. "Don't expect me to be here when you get back."

"Suit yourself," he said without emotion. He walked across the room, passing her as if she weren't there, and went out the door. That was the last time she'd seen him.

For two long years. Until now. Until this tumultuous evening in Austin.

She stared at him, sitting so at ease across from her, the hint of a mocking smile at the corner of his mouth, the mischief back in his eyes. She hated that he could still awaken desire in her, but this time she knew it for what it was.

Sex was all we ever had, she told herself coldly. *And it wasn't enough. Everything else was illusion. We weren't soul mates, only bedmates.*

This time his charm wouldn't fool her, she knew too well what it hid—a self-destructive man who loved danger more than he could ever love her.

JAKE HAD MEANT what he'd said. She was as beautiful as ever, perhaps even more so. Her dark hair spilled down like a thick, shimmering curtain of silk. He thought it was impossible for a man to look at that wealth of lustrous hair and not want to touch it.

Her features were lovely, but he had loved them not simply for their beauty, but for the spirit that shone through them. Soul mates, she had once called the two of them, and he'd felt it had been true. He was an expert at disguising his emotions, too good at it perhaps, but she'd never mastered the art.

He used to tease her that she had a face made of glass, that he could see right through it to whatever she was thinking. At this moment he could see how much it cost her to accept help from him. She must be desperate, he thought. Completely desperate.

"All right," he said as gently as he could. "You and I were too different to make things work. You don't like what I do. But I'm still a detective—and a good one. Now you want to tell me about your aunt?"

Julie swallowed and stared down at the pale green tablecloth. "It's like I told you on the phone. She disappeared seven weeks ago—almost eight. She'd come here to Austin for a teachers' workshop. But then she—just vanished. The police can't find any trace of her. And I'm afraid—I'm afraid—"

She stopped and bit her lip, still keeping her eyes down. Jake knew that look by heart. It meant she was trying not to cry; she hated to cry.

She'd set aside the menu, and her left hand lay clenched in a tense fist on the tabletop. Impulsively he put his hand over hers, squeezing it. "It's okay. Tell me at your own pace," he said.

She cast an unhappy glance at their joined hands. "I don't want you to touch me," she said from between her teeth. "I told you that. That was part of the agreement."

Reluctantly he moved his hand. It tingled from touching her, filling him with hunger to touch her more.

She shook her head. "You shouldn't have kissed me, either. Don't do it again."

That kiss had made him a little crazy for a moment, feeling her lips, warm and almost pliant beneath his. Maybe it had made him very crazy; he couldn't tell anymore.

"Fine," he said with false carelessness. "I kissed you hello, that's all. If I get the job done, you can kiss me goodbye. We'll be even. But in the meantime, the important thing is your aunt. Her name is—Becky Albert?"

Julie crumpled the dark green linen napkin in a nervous motion. "Rebecca. Nobody ever called her Becky. I'm afraid. My whole family thinks—that something bad's happened to her."

She kept toying with the napkin, then her hands went still and she raised her eyes to him. They were wonderful brown eyes, so gorgeous they always knocked his heart askew. Now they were bright with unshed tears.

"I told you on the phone," she said, trying to control her voice. "Two other women have disappeared in Austin. Their b-bodies have been found. The police think—think it's a serial killer."

He nodded, cool and professional. "But you said the other two women were different. Younger. In their twenties. And Becky—Rebecca's fifty."

Julie made a helpless gesture. "But that's no comfort, is it? I mean, some serial killers have a pattern, but others don't. If anybody's harmed her, I couldn't stand it. She never hurt anybody in her life. And the police are doing nothing—nothing at all."

He chose his words carefully, trying to make it as easy as he could. "Julie, missing person cases are the hardest to solve. And you said, there's only one lead. The night she disappeared, she was seen in the hotel restaurant—with a man, right?"

"Yes. One of the waiters there remembers her. She was with a man wearing a ball cap and 'a lot of turquoise rings.' That's exactly what the waiter said, 'a *lot* of turquoise rings.' They had a drink together. Then they left. And nobody's seen her since."

She tossed her head rebelliously. "The police need to find this man. They should be combing the state for him. Why haven't they, dammit?"

He wished he could offer her some magic answer that would solve everything and bring back Rebecca Albert, safe and sound. But he couldn't. "You say she wasn't the type to pick up a stranger?"

"Absolutely not," Julie said with conviction. "It's totally out of character. She's a very conservative woman, and she hardly ever drank. She must have known this man from somewhere—she *had* to, or she wouldn't have been with him. But the police aren't even trying to find him. And it makes me angry, Jake."

Better angry than mourning, Jake thought. Grief could paralyze you, but anger could keep you going long after everything else failed.

"Somebody has to do something," she said defiantly, "even if it's only me,"

"So you hired the private detective you told me about," he said.

"Yes. But I might as well have thrown my money in the Perdenales River. He didn't find anything. And he cost me a thousand dollars."

She'd gone pale when she'd started talking about her aunt. But remembering the private detective brought a vivid flush to her cheeks. That was his Julie, he thought with a dart of pain, so full of emotion.

"A lot of private eyes say they can find a missing person," he said. "Damned few can deliver. They run a few standard traces and give up. The truth is, they don't know how to go further."

"That's exactly what he did," Julie said with contempt. "He did stupid things. He checked the post office to see if she'd put in a forwarding address, for God's sake."

"Yeah," Jake said. "Stuff like that."

"Then he contacted the bank," she said. "To see if she'd transferred any money before she disappeared. And a credit agency, to see if she'd run up some enormous debts or something."

"And he found nothing out of the ordinary, right?"

"Of course not," Julie said, clenching her fist again. "He acted as if *she* was guilty of something. When I asked him about the man with the turquoise rings, he had the nerve to say to me, 'A lot of guys wear too much turquoise, lady. It'd be like looking for a needle in a haystack.'"

"That's when you fired him?" He almost smiled. He could imagine the passion and flair she'd brought to that little job.

"Yes. But then I didn't know where to turn."

"So you turned to me." He wasn't flattered; he knew better than that. She was telling the truth, as always. She'd phoned him because he was her last resort, it was that clear and simple.

"So I turned to you," she said, the color once more fading from her face. "Because I don't know where she is or what's happened to her. If she's like those other women— What if she's lying out there somewhere, abandoned? She always hated the cold, and it's been such a cold spring...to think of her in the dark and the cold like tonight—"

This time, she couldn't force the tears back. She dashed them away angrily with the edge of her hand. He ached to hold her, but he made no move to touch her.

The waiter appeared, hovering over them, all unctuous smiles and politeness. "Do you wish to order now? Or perhaps you'd like more time? I could make a suggestion, if you'd like. The fajitas supremas are our specialty—"

"I'm not hungry," Julie said, furiously scrubbing the last tear away. "You," she said, throwing Jake a determined look, "you order whatever you want. I told you I'd pay your expenses while you're here."

"I'm not hungry, either," he said, pushing his chair back. "Come on. Let's get out of here."

She looked disconcerted. "But—I'm fine. I just got a little misty."

"No. Let's split." To the startled waiter he said, *"La cuenta, por favor?"*

The waiter quickly wrote out their bill. Jake slapped a ten-dollar bill on the table, seized Julie by the elbow and steered her toward the restaurant's front door.

"I'm supposed to pay," she said, looking back at the table.

"I'll run a tab," he said grimly, and shouldered open the door. The April night was chilly and had started to mist. He put on his Stetson, then pulled down the brim. "Where's your car?"

"Over there. In the lot. The silver Chevy. Look, I didn't mean to go weepy on you. I'm *not* a weak person."

"Nobody knows that better than I do," he said. "Come on."

"But where? That homicide detective you know—can we see him tonight?"

"No," he said. "First thing tomorrow morning. Which hotel are you staying in? The same one your aunt did?"

"Yes. I thought we could ask some questions."

"You got me a room there, too?"

"Yes. I told you I would."

"Not the same as yours, I suppose." He shouldn't have asked the question, but he couldn't resist.

"Absolutely not," she said, her chin jerking up. "I'm on the top floor. You're on the bottom."

He almost said, *I always liked it when you were on the top. Remember that time in Oklahoma City, when we . . .*

He kept his mouth shut.

They stopped beside her car, and she retrieved her keys from her purse without fumbling. She opened the door, then hit the button to the passenger's side.

"Get in," she said.

He slid into the seat, glancing into the back. It was cluttered with art supplies, just as he remembered.

She put the car in gear, then backed out of the lot with speed and verve. She was a bold driver, with no timidness in her.

They rode for a block in silence, and he studied the strange, futuristic skyline of downtown Austin. This was where she'd grown up, but she didn't live here. Her little house was some sixty miles to the west, in the heart of the rolling hill country.

"Were you going to meet your aunt while she was in Austin?" he asked.

"No. I was on assignment in Mexico. Cozumel."

"You didn't see her often?"

Julie shook her head. "Only once or twice a year. I was raised here. She's from out around Odessa, in the Panhandle."

She hesitated, giving him a measured sidelong glance. "I have to say something to you."

"Yes?"

She turned her attention from him and drew to a halt for a red light. The mist had turned to rain, and she switched on the windshield wipers.

She took a deep breath. "I didn't ask you to come, you know. When I phoned you, all I wanted was advice. You talk just as fast as you always did. Before I knew what was happening, you said you were coming. It was your idea, not mine."

He glanced at her profile. She still held her chin high, and her hands firmly gripped on the wheel, as if she were in complete control of it and her destiny.

"You don't need advice," he said. "You need a real detective. Not one who got his badge by mail order. I've got a connection or two down here. They'll tell me things they wouldn't tell you. I'm not doing this for money. You don't have to reimburse me. I don't want it."

The light turned green, and she accelerated. "I said I'd pay your expenses. That includes your plane fare. I want a complete statement when this is over. With receipts."

"And when this is over, we're going to sit down and talk about you and me."

"There's nothing to talk about. You can't negotiate emotions," she said. "I thought I made that clear."

"I'll keep my word," he said, pulling down his hat brim a notch more. "I won't try to touch you again. If that's what you want."

"It's what I want."

He leaned against the seat and gave a short laugh. "It's funny. Two years ago you didn't want me because I was a cop. Now that's the only reason you do. Ain't life strange?"

She shot him a defiant glance. "Do we need all this talk about wanting? I want only one thing. To find my aunt. And if anything's happened to her—"

Her voice had gone a little shaky again. He thought, darkly, that suspected murder created a lousy atmosphere for wooing back a lost love.

"If anything's happened to her, then what?" he asked.

She paused a moment before answering, staring out at the road. "Then I want you to find me the man with the turquoise rings."

He weighed this for a moment. "You know that we may not find anything, don't you? The odds *are* against us."

"It's a chance I have to take," she said.

"Even if it means bringing me into the picture?" he added, letting a taunt creep into his voice.

"Yes," she said, giving him a steely look. "Even that, Good Thunder. Even that."

He held her gaze a moment. "I still want you, you know."

"Tough luck," she answered and turned her attention back to the road. "I don't make the same mistakes twice."

2

As THEY ENTERED the hotel, Julie's stomach twisted. She felt haunted and slightly sick. Seven and a half weeks ago, Rebecca had crossed this lobby, then vanished.

Had this place, with its cold, modern decor, its chrome and Plexiglas and imitation marble, been what Rebecca had seen on what might have been the last night of her life?

Jake nodded toward the stark marble arch that led into the hotel's main restaurant. "The waiter who saw her," he asked, "is he on duty tonight?"

Julie nodded numbly. "Yes. He doesn't work full-time. He's a student. I've talked to him twice. He insists he's told everything he remembers to the police. Actually, he was pretty snippy about it."

"Nobody else at the hotel remembers the man with the turquoise rings?"

"No. Nobody."

"Then let's go see our waiter friend. Maybe I can improve his memory."

Jake took her arm, tucking it securely in his. Physical awareness, strong and seductive, swarmed through her. Almost involuntarily, she glanced up and met his dark eyes.

He smiled his easy one-cornered smile, as if he knew he still wielded some of his old power over her. *Damn him*, she thought.

"You don't have to hold on to me, Good Thunder," she said coldly.

"It gives us a psychological advantage. It shows you're in my hands, that I'm your protector, your hired gun, so to speak."

She rolled her eyes. "Hired gun? Spare me."

"I'll do most of the talking. Look aloof, like you're in charge of it all, and I'm the guy who does the dirty work."

He stopped between one of the restaurant's marble pillars and a large potted palm. "You'll do better at looking aloof if your lipstick isn't smeared."

He raised his free hand to her face and gently wiped the corner of her mouth with his thumb, a slow teasing motion.

She was taken aback by how pleasurable, how exciting she found that simple movement. But she got hold of herself. "Back off, Jake. I mean it. I want you to find my aunt, not mend my makeup."

His hand dropped away, settling on his tooled belt, his thumb hooking next to the silver buckle. "How about me?" he asked mildly. "Am I carrying any of your war paint?"

She narrowed her eyes because she did see a faint smudge of rosy-red just at the edge of his lower lip. "Yes," she said, and pointed to the same spot on her own mouth. "Right there. Wipe it off."

He kept his eyes fixed on her lips as he ran the tip of his tongue over his lower lip, then drew his knuckle across it. "There." He smiled. "Am I decent?"

"I doubt if you'll ever be that," she said.

"Good," he said. "Very good. Keep that expression. Nose in the air. Haughty."

She didn't dignify the comment with an answer.

"All right. You say this guy's name is Kevin Waring? Point him out when we get inside."

She gave him a curt nod. Arm in arm with Jake, she entered the restaurant, and it gave her the same haunted, empty feeling she experienced in the lobby. Where had Rebecca gone when she'd left here? What could have become of her?

The dining room was large but stark. More chrome, more Plexiglas, more flawless plants born and bred in a greenhouse, protected from the realities of nature.

Julie's eyes swept around the room. The walls were painted in the trite pastels that had come to signify commercial southwest decor. The light, neither too bright nor too dim, fell from gleaming geometrical fixtures.

Few people were dining; it was growing past the supper hour. Tables stood empty, covered with stark white linen, set with sterile perfection. Recorded music, mellow and utterly forgettable, played softly.

A tall, lean young man came from the kitchen to a table occupied by an elderly couple. With a long-suffering expression on his face, he refilled their wineglasses, then strolled toward the cash register, his gait as languid and self-assured as a cat's.

"Him," Julie whispered, nodding. "That's Kevin Waring."

She stole a glance at Jake. In mere seconds, his face had transformed. Playfulness no longer touched his eyes or lips. He radiated an air of such utter relentlessness it startled her. Was this another mask? Or the real Jake?

When Kevin Waring glanced up and saw Jake's gaze on him, his expression changed. For a moment he no longer looked arrogant or disdainful. He was only a handsome but lanky college boy dressed up in a tuxedo that didn't quite fit.

"Waring?" Jake asked. His voice was a cool rasp.

The young man seemed rooted to the spot as Jake and Julie neared him. He was fair-haired, with smooth skin, even features and sapphire eyes. He did not smile.

Jake let go of Julie's arm, took a wallet from the back pocket of his jeans, flipped it open and flashed a badge at Waring.

"Detective Sergeant Jacob Good Thunder, Oklahoma State Police," Jake said in the same low, gravelly voice. "I'm helping Miss FitzJames investigate the disappearance of Rebecca Albert."

Waring's nostrils flared as he gazed at the badge. He seemed to force himself into composure. His mouth took on the superior, sarcastic line Julie remembered with distaste.

"Oklahoma?" Waring said dubiously. "How did the Oklahoma police get mixed up in this?"

"I'll ask the questions, Mr. Waring. You saw Rebecca Albert in this dining room on the night of February sixteenth?"

Waring crossed his arms. "Yes. Overweight little woman with a round face, a bad perm and a kind of limp. Middle-aged, plain. Did you come to show me another picture? Have at it. Little did I know this would be my life's work."

Julie bristled at Waring's tone and his cruel description of Rebecca. Jake might have taken the young man by surprise at first, but Waring had returned to his old, unpleasant self with amazing speed.

"How about it?" Jake said to Julie. "Did you bring another picture?"

"Yes." She snapped open her purse, pulled out an envelope and withdrew a snapshot.

In the photo, Rebecca stood on the porch of her little house she had lived in all her life. On one side of her hung a bird feeder, on the other a wicker basket of cascading petunias. She stood in between them, smiling guilelessly at the camera.

Julie handed the picture to Waring, who studied it without enthusiasm. "That's her," he said. "She looks better with her hair straight. And she sat right *there*."

He stabbed his finger in the direction of a corner table. "Do you wonder how I remember?" he asked Jake, a sneer in his voice. "They didn't leave a tip. They sat in that corner during the supper rush for two bloody hours, tying up the table. She nursed one glass of white wine, and he had two beers."

Julie frowned slightly. She hadn't heard this part of the story before. "Nobody left a tip?" she asked. "Who paid the bill?"

Waring handed the snapshot back to her and crossed his arms again. "I don't know. And the cashier doesn't remember. *She* was having boyfriend problems, as usual. I thought I went through all this."

"Tell me about the man Rebecca was with," Jake said.

Waring gave an extravagant sigh. "Medium height, stocky build. Blue jeans, the boxy kind that fat guys wear. Denim jacket, ball cap with some kind of animal on it."

"What kind of animal?" Jake asked.

Waring shrugged. "I don't know. I thought it was a sports cap, like for a team. With a badger or a wolverine or a wombat or something on it. I don't *know* anything about sports, for God's sake. Or our furry friends."

Jake set his jaw. He put his arm around Julie's shoulders as if to tell Waring he intended to take care of her, very good care. "Suppose you tell us what you *do* know, Mr. Waring. You're a student? What's your field?"

Waring seemed startled by the question. "Me? European history—why?"

"I said I'll do the asking. The man—how old was he?"

"He was one of those guys who could have been any-where from thirty-five to fifty-five," Waring said testily.

"What about his coloring, his features, how he carried himself?"

"I can't tell you about his hair, he kept on the cap. His gait? He walked the way a fat guy walks. He was nonde-script. Totally. Except for the rings. He wore a lot of tur-quoise rings. Enough to look tacky. That was the only noticeable thing about him, the rings."

"How did he and the woman act together?" Jake asked. "Like lovers? Old friends? Or like they were just getting acquainted?"

Waring shook his head. "She acted a little—animated. More than he did. Almost coquettish. Or maybe that's just her way."

Julie objected. "No. It wasn't. She was shy, never co-quettish. Rebecca used to be—"

She broke off, horrified. She had been speaking of Re-becca in the past tense as if her aunt were dead and gone forever. She bit her lip.

Jake's arm tightened around her shoulders. To Waring, he said, "If you remember anything else, anything at all, get in touch with me. Understand? Here's my card."

He reached into his shirt pocket and withdrew a card. Wordlessly he offered it, and wordlessly Kevin Waring took it.

A tense look, fraught with challenge, passed between the men. Julie felt it, strong as a charge of electricity, and her nerve endings prickled.

"Will that be all?" Waring asked, his blue eyes trained on Jake, frosty but steady.

"For now," Jake said.

Waring turned and left, padding swiftly and silently towards the kitchen, disappearing through its swinging doors.

Julie's heart hammered in her chest. Jake's nearness didn't help, so she shrugged off his arm and marched back to the lobby. She stopped, turned and let him catch up.

"What was *that?*" she demanded, puzzled. "He acted almost scared of you at first. Something happened in there between you—what? Do you think he's lying?"

"I don't think he's telling the whole truth."

"Why?"

He gave her his one-cornered smile. "Call it instinct. Did he say anything you didn't know before?"

She put her fingertips to her throbbing temple. "Yes. That nobody left a tip. That's not like Rebecca. She was always a generous person—too generous, in fact."

"Anything else?"

Julie massaged her temple. "Yes. Rebecca acting coquettish. That's not her style. He must be wrong."

"Wrong or lying. I want to check up on Waring. In the meantime, you look like you could use a drink."

He nodded toward an open door on the far side of the lobby. Over the door a neon sign flashed the invitation: Welcome To Pecos Billy's.

"Want to try the bar?" he asked.

She felt emotionally exhausted, yet too keyed up to sleep. A drink would be good. A drink would help.

"Not here," she said. "This place makes me think of Rebecca. I keep imagining—I don't even want to say what I imagine. I wish I hadn't booked us rooms here."

"We don't have to stay," he said, his mouth close to her ear. "We could go somewhere else."

His voice was kind, but it was full of intimate suggestion, as well. She stepped away from him as if he were poison. She glanced at him resentfully, wondering what was going through his mind, his quick, agile, devious mind.

"There's a bar a couple of blocks down the street," she said. "The Wagon Spoke. It's honky-tonk, live music, sawdust on the floor and beer in long-necked bottles. We'll go there. I'll tell you more about my aunt. While we drink two beers, no more. Then we come back here. And go our separate ways until morning."

For the space of three heartbeats, his dark gaze held hers, and there it was—the old magic working full force again, exciting and mesmerizing.

If he'd held out his hand to her and said, "No. Let's go upstairs. You need to be held, and I need to hold you—"

If he had said that, she would have gone, God help her.

But he said nothing, only kept staring into her eyes as if he couldn't understand what he saw there. Then the moment passed.

Sanity returned. Two years ago, she'd gotten off the crazy and dangerous carnival ride of loving him. She was determined never to get on again.

He shoved his hands into the back pockets of his jeans and said, "Okay. Let's hit the honky-tonk and talk about your aunt. That's why I'm here."

She ignored the humming in her blood. She snapped her purse open smartly and drew out her car keys.

"Fine. Let's go," she said, tossing her hair. "And remember, I'm buying. I pay your way."

"Because you're the boss lady here?"

"You can think of it that way," she said.

He smiled. "We'll see," he said.

THE WAGON SPOKE was one of those dark, ancient, ramshackle little bars that had no glamour whatsoever but enough personality to outclass a hundred bars like the hotel's charmless Pecos Billy's.

On the small stage, which listed to one side rather alarmingly, stood a slim woman playing a guitar. She stood in the spotlight, her head thrown back, singing with all her heart about love gone wrong.

Jake gave the singer a sardonic look. She was too young and appeared to be too happy to understand about love really gone wrong, so wrong you might lose it forever.

He sat with Julie at a table that wobbled because of an unsteady leg. Around them, cowboys and would-be cowboys sat in the dim light with their ladies.

In a far corner, two men in cowboy hats played the Dolly Parton pinball machine, ornamented with a large picture of Dolly herself, all blond hair, bosom and sass.

It was a Friday night with a fine, warm, life-giving spring rain drumming down outside. The music was good, the beer was cold and everybody seemed happy and full of hell-raising fun. All except Jake, who pretended to be as content as anyone, and Julie, of course, who was never good at pretending anything.

She hardly touched her beer and wouldn't eat, even though he offered to share his cheeseburger and fries.

"That stuff's not good for you," she said, looking glumly at the juicy sandwich and the plate heaped with hot, oily curlycue fries. "If you keep eating like that, it'll kill you."

"Sooner or later, something'll kill me, that's for sure," he said, eating another fry. "This is soul food for a cop. I need my Vitamin G."

"Vitamin G?" she said dubiously.

"Vitamin Grease. Can't be happy unless you get a little Vitamin G every now and then."

She tried to smile, but didn't quite succeed. Her beautiful Bambi-eyes looked at him sadly. "You're hopelessly self-indulgent," she said, but there was no rancor in her voice.

"Yup," he said cheerfully.

No, he thought dolefully. If he was really self-indulgent, he'd stand up, kick the table out of the way and throw her over his shoulder. Then he'd carry her back to the hotel, and make love to her until the earth spun out of orbit.

Lord, he thought, there'd been more than a few times back in Oklahoma when he'd believed they'd done it. They'd made love until the planet seemed knocked loose from gravity, spinning dizzily through a whole new galaxy.

"Let's not enumerate my faults," he said. "Let's talk about Rebecca. I hardly remember you talking about an aunt when you were in Oklahoma. You never mentioned her much."

She put her chin on her cupped hands and gazed at the people on the dance floor. Lean-hipped cowboys led their partners around the floor, whirling and darting.

"All right," Julie said, not looking at him. "I'll confess something. I feel guilty about Rebecca . . . I really do. It took so little to make her happy. I should have gone to see her more often."

"You mean, you're doing this out of guilt? Not exactly the purest of motives, brown-eyes."

She sighed and straightened up, looking pensively at her beer bottle. "It's not just guilt. If she'd dropped from a heart attack or something, I'd feel just as guilty as I do now—no more, no less. I was always so busy living my own life. And we were hundreds of miles apart. I tried to call her once a month or so. Why didn't I do it more often?"

Julie took a deep breath. "And, to tell you the truth, she was a bit hard to talk to. Not when I was a child. But when

I grew up, she seemed to change toward me. I don't think she was ever really comfortable with adults."

"But you stayed in touch?"

"I tried. I could get her to talk, if I worked at it. Once she relaxed, she was lovely—sweet and open and, I thought, happy. I should have tried to make her happy more often. So I feel guilty."

"And?" he prompted.

She squared her chin. "All right. I also feel angry. Angry at the police, angry at the whole system. Rebecca's gone, but nobody seems to *care*. A sweet, gentle woman is gone, and nobody's doing a thing. It's not right. I can't let her be overlooked like that."

He tried to comfort her without sounding patronizing. "Like I told you, a missing person case is a tough call. Especially if it's an adult that's missing. Thousands of people go away—they've planned to disappear. Most of them show up again sooner or later. It happens all the time."

Julie's chin jerked up rebelliously. "That's the standard police answer, and you know it. Rebecca *didn't* plan to disappear. Everything points to exactly the opposite. I told you so on the phone."

Pushing away his plate, he sighed and leaned back in his chair, like a man settling in for a long conversation.

"Okay, Julie," he said with a patient nod. "On the phone you gave me the short version. Tell me in detail. Spare nothing. The night's young."

How does the song go? he thought, taking in the way the light gleamed on her long hair. *Something about the night being young, and you being beautiful.*

He gave himself a mental kick. She didn't want him as a lover, she wanted him as a cop. He must stop coveting her beguiling mouth and her soft, smooth body.

"First, there's her job," Julie said finally, squaring her shoulders. "She's a kindergarten teacher, and she's been in her town's school system since she graduated from college—twenty-eight years. In that whole time, she never missed a day, unless she was seriously ill. Not a single day, Jake. Now, with no explanation, she's missed almost eight weeks."

He put his hand to his chin and rubbed his upper lip thoughtfully. "Okay. What else?"

"Plenty else," Julie said with conviction. "She was full of plans. Her car, for one thing. She'd had her old Ford for twelve years. She'd just ordered a new one, with custom color, a cassette player, and a whole bunch of other special features. She was so excited."

"Go on."

Julie frowned in concentration. "Then there's her dog. Her old dog died last spring. It was a cocker spaniel, seventeen years old. At first she wouldn't even consider getting another dog. But then she changed her mind. Another teacher had a French bulldog she'd bred. There were going to be pups. Rebecca was supposed to get the pick of the litter. She was walking on air over that, too."

Jake lifted a quizzical eyebrow. "A French bulldog? I never heard of such a thing. What's it do? Wear a little beret and eat snails?"

Julie smiled, but her smile was pensive. "No. It's a funny little dog with ears like a bat. But quiet. It doesn't need a lot of exercise. A good dog for an older person."

"Rebecca wasn't that old."

"Fifty," Julie said. "There are people who are young at fifty, and people who are old."

"True."

"I don't mean to sound cruel," Julie said earnestly. "Rebecca was very set in her ways. She has been all her life.

That's another reason why she wouldn't disappear voluntarily. She was a creature of habit."

Her obvious concern touched him. Julie was passionate about the people she loved, sometimes passionate to a fault, but what she said made perfect sense. Still, his job was to play devil's advocate.

He said, "Let me see that picture of her, will you?"

Julie picked up her purse, opened it and handed him the envelope with the picture.

For a moment, her fingers, slim and warm, touched his. It was if she'd sent a lightning bolt coursing through him that split and simultaneously struck both his mind and his groin.

Steady, he told himself. But he noticed that she'd snatched her hand back as if she'd felt something, too.

He took the picture and willed himself to concentrate. Rebecca Albert bore no resemblance whatsoever to her beautiful niece.

Rebecca was short and plump, a soft little dumpling of a woman. Julie's brown eyes were full of feminine mystery, but Rebecca's were blue and as innocent as a child's.

In the photo, her round, unremarkable face was tilted slightly, and her only notable feature was her hair. It was gray, straight and smoothly drawn back into some sort of braid or bun.

Jake studied the picture, then gave Julie a quizzical frown. "Kevin Waring said something about her hair. He mentioned it twice, in fact. He said she looked better in straight hair. And that she had a bad perm. She changed her hair from this?"

Julie toyed with a strand of her own ebony hair. "Last autumn, before school started, she decided long hair was too much work. She had it cut off and permed. I wish she hadn't."

"The experiment wasn't a success?"

"I didn't think so," Julie said. "But I'd never seen her with short hair before. She liked it, and that's what counted."

Jake raised an eyebrow dubiously. "Waring also said she walked with a limp. Why? Has she always limped?"

Julie shook her head. "No. It developed a while back, but it got really bad last winter. She thought it was arthritis. I tried to talk her into seeing a doctor. She wouldn't. She was stubborn about things like that."

Jake rubbed his upper lip again and studied the picture harder. "And she left home to come to Austin for a teachers' workshop?"

Just then, the young singer in the spotlight began to wail about lost chances, lost loves and lost youth. Julie pushed her hair back from her shoulder. "A teachers' meeting, yes. Jake, I can't sit here like this. I'm too nervous. Could we dance or something?"

His heart seemed to fall down an elevator shaft. Hold her in his arms? But go no further? She would have been kinder to draw out a gun and shoot him.

"Sure," he said gruffly.

She was out of her chair before he could pull it back and help her. She reached the edge of the dance floor before he did, then turned to him, holding her arms out stiffly.

He went to her as if they were a pair of magnets, fated to attract, but she held him firmly at a distance. He took her hand in his, put his other hand on her waist and led her onto the floor.

They kept in step with each other effortlessly; their bodies had always worked together perfectly, at dancing and sex. Was she doing this to torment him?

"Let me hold you closer," he said from between his teeth. "This far apart, I feel like an eighth-grader who's afraid of girls."

She gave him a cynical look. "I doubt if you were ever afraid of girls. And we're here to talk about Rebecca."

He moved his hand higher up her back so he could feel the silkiness of her hair brush his skin. "All right. She came to Austin for a teachers' meeting."

He whirled her around, hoping to distract her enough to draw her closer, and succeeding. He lessened the distance between them by several inches. She didn't seem to notice. He almost smiled.

"School was out that Friday because it's some town holiday, Founder's Day or something."

"And the town is . . . ?"

"Casino. Between Amarillo and Lubbock. The teachers' conference was one day, that Saturday, but it's a long round-trip to Austin and back. So Rebecca came a day early to do some shopping."

Julie paused, her expression thoughtful and worried. "And she did shop. They found everything she bought, still in the bags, lying on the dresser in her hotel room. But her bed had never been slept in."

"What had she bought?" he asked.

Julie looked positively stricken. "She was buying winter clothes for the next school year. She always hit the end-of-winter sales to save money. She'd bought a new skirt, two new blouses and a pair of shoes. She'd even put a down payment on a new winter coat."

She looked up at him with that pleading look that drove him half-crazy. "See, Jake? Doesn't that prove it? If she was planning to disappear, why would she be buying clothes for next winter?"

"I don't know, sugar," he said. "That's a good point." Without thinking, he had let one of his many pet names for her slip out. But she hadn't seemed to notice.

Her forehead creased and she shook her head. "She left her car sitting in the hotel parking lot. If she went anywhere, how did she get there?"

"I don't know," he repeated. The music let him whirl her again, and he took advantage of the opportunity to draw her closer still. She was so caught up in her thoughts of Rebecca, she made no objection.

"She'd taken nothing from her bank account," Julie mused aloud, staring into space.

"Another thing," she said. "She left her prescription medicine on the sink counter in the bathroom. Driving and strange situations gave her anxiety attacks. She wouldn't go anywhere without her medication."

She went silent a moment. Her body moved with the music, but her mind, he could tell, was far away.

When she spoke again, her voice was tight. "You know what the worst thing is? She left her houseplants with nobody to water them. She'd mail-ordered flowers for her garden, too. The plants came but she wasn't there. She wouldn't go off and let that happen. She *loved* her flowers. But now they're all—dead. She'd hate that. She'd never do that on purpose."

The tempo of the music changed to a slow, romantic number. He pulled her closer, the way they used to dance. At the same time, he said, "How do know about the houseplants dying?"

He thought she'd draw back, but she didn't. "I got into the house," she said. "I knew where she kept the spare key. The boxes with the mail-order plants were outside her door. I opened them."

"And?" he coaxed. She was deliciously close, and he could smell her perfume, the clean scent of lily-of-the-valley.

"When I saw those plants, it—it was like an evil omen. They were all withered in their plastic pots. And for the first time, I got really scared. I knew Rebecca would never, ever let that happen."

"And the houseplants?" he asked.

"That was even worse," she said with feeling. "Her African violets—her ferns—all dead. When I saw that, I wanted to cry. She's gone, Jake, but she didn't go on purpose. Something's happened to her, I know it."

It was not his imagination; she was holding him tighter, now. She lay her cheek against his shoulder, and he wondered if she could feel the thunderous pounding of his heart.

The music stopped, so he stopped moving. For a moment, they simply held each other. He didn't want to scare her off by kissing her, but the temptation grew almost too keen to bear. He tried not to get drunk on her touch, her fragrance. He allowed himself to brush his lips against her hair, so lightly he knew she could not feel it.

Then somebody put coins in the jukebox and some moron began to yowl a song about Bubba shooting the jukebox on Saturday night because the music made him sad. The singer on stage had finished her set, and abruptly the lights came on.

Julie drew back from him with the expression of a sleepwalker who's just awakened. Jake damned the light and felt like shooting the jukebox himself.

He gave her a small smile meant to be ironic. "It was almost like old times for a second, hmm?"

But she didn't smile back. She looked bewildered and maybe a little bit angry, whether at herself or him or both, he didn't know. Then her face took on an expression of anxiety again.

"Something's happened to Rebecca," she said. "The police won't believe me. Will you?"

His hand still rested on her back, grazed softly by the midnight cascade of her hair. His other hand still held hers, but tentatively, as if he couldn't move nearer to her without something fragile between them breaking.

He wanted to pull her against him again, lower his mouth to hers and drink her in until they both were dizzy from the passion. But he stayed where he was, using all the self-discipline he could muster.

"Yes," he said. "I believe you."

He didn't know if that was true, only that it was what she needed to hear.

She looked up at him with a hint of her old spirit dancing in her eyes. "Thanks, Jake. That means a lot to me."

"Think nothing of it," he said, and when she moved away from him, he let her go without protest.

3

THEY DROVE BACK to the hotel through the rain, making small talk.

"It's been a wet spring," she said.

"Has it?"

"Yes. But the wildflowers are coming out."

"Are they?"

"They're beautiful this year. This part of Texas is famous for its wildflowers."

"Is it?"

"Yes. It is."

She was grateful when they reached the hotel. He wanted to escort her to her room, but she refused. She knew where it would lead.

First, he'd ask to come in—just for a few moments—and it would be too easy for her to say yes. A few moments would turn into all night; all night would turn into a new affair; a new affair would be just as disastrous as the old one, and she couldn't bear that kind of pain again.

She looked up at him, wishing she could be immune to the yearning he stirred in her. She said, "I'll be fine."

"Rebecca wasn't," he said.

She turned from him and pushed the elevator button. "I won't be far off. I'm on the eighth floor."

"Yeah," he said. "And I'm down here. You're on the top and I'm on the bottom."

She blushed and hated herself for doing it. She was grateful when the elevator doors sighed open.

He put out his hand as if to detain her, then stopped himself. "Good night, Julie," he said flatly.

"Good night," she said and stepped inside the elevator. She hit the button for her floor. Like theater curtains, the doors slid shut, cutting off her view of Jake.

Leaning against the wall, she closed her eyes, but his image still burned vividly in her mind. *A tall man with an easy stance and a white Stetson tipped at a rakish angle. A body made for action. Dark eyes that could gaze with cool mockery or hot passion. A mouth meant for laughter and kissing...*

"Oh, hell," she muttered. The elevator stopped, and she got out, went down the carpeted hall and unlocked her door.

She'd booked the same room that Rebecca had taken in February. Rebecca had reserved it—but never slept in it. She'd left behind all her belongings, old and new. For the thousandth time, Julie worried what terrible thing had befallen her aunt.

She slid the chain lock into place, then went to the window, pushed aside the white drape and stared out at the rainy night.

Had Rebecca, too, looked out this window, stared at this view? The downtown lights were blurry in the distance, but a lighted billboard across the street was clear and stark: In The Midst Of Life We Are In Death. This message brought to you by the Prism Street Church of Deliverance.

Julie let the drape fall back into place and turned away. Each day her aunt was gone, Julie lost more hope. This hotel room seemed like her last link to her aunt, and its silence, its cold decor told her nothing, nothing at all.

She lay on the bed, wondering if Rebecca had stretched out on it to rest after her day of shopping, before she met the man with the turquoise rings. Julie put her hand up to cover her eyes, which burned with unshed tears.

If it was humanly possible to find Rebecca, Jake would find her. Julie believed this with all her heart. But she'd found that this same all-too-human heart ached almost as much from Jake's presence as it did from Rebecca's absence.

When he'd said he would come to help her, she'd been both elated and frightened. Now that he was here, her mind clamored that she must keep her distance, but her heart and body sent out traitorous, contrary signals.

Eyes closed, she wondered bleakly why she'd told him she wanted to dance. She had, in truth, been restless. And she'd wanted to prove to herself that he was only a man like any other—she'd been so caught up in her concern for Rebecca, she'd almost succeeded in convincing herself.

But now the memory of his nearness, his arms around her, haunted her, and so did his words: "I still want you."

I still want you.

She sat up, rebuking herself. Loving him had been the royal road to heartbreak and she wouldn't travel it again.

"Been there, done that," she told herself with disdain. She rose and went to take a long, cold shower.

THE OFFICE OF Detective Sergeant Paco Martinez was a crowded cubbyhole, its walls hidden by bookshelves, file cabinets and bulletin boards.

Martinez was a trim, handsome man with a slightly pitted complexion and a black mustache. He wore a pale blue oxford-cloth shirt pressed to perfection, a precisely knotted tie and a shoulder holster containing a nasty-looking gun.

The detective sergeant sat behind his desk, which was littered with papers, heaped with file folders and cluttered with an array of objects: a telephone, pocket calculator, stapler, coffee mug, notebook, scissors, a holder crammed with pencils and pens, and framed snapshots.

The room hardly had space for two more chairs, but he managed to wedge them in. Julie sat uncomfortably close to Jake, and their knees kept touching.

"Miss FitzJames," Martinez said, "I'm sorry, but as far as finding your aunt, we've hit a brick wall. We're waiting for a break in the case. One will come, I believe this. But it's a matter of luck. For now, all we can do is be patient."

Julie's temper simmered dangerously. "I was taught that the harder you work, the luckier you get. Breaks come when you go out and look for them."

Jake gave her a sharp look, but Martinez's answer was mild. "The case is still open. We have an all-points bulletin out. Other jurisdictions have been notified."

"Yes," Julie retorted. "But that was done seven weeks ago. I want to know what's being done *now*."

Martinez sighed and scratched his mustache. Jake shifted in his chair, bringing his thigh against Julie's. She tried to edge away, but couldn't.

"Paco," Jake said, "what about the connection between Rebecca Albert and this serial killer?"

A shudder rippled up Julie's spine, but she steeled her nerves and forced herself to look at Martinez.

His face remained calm, implacable. "Frankly, she doesn't fit his pattern. The other two women were young, in their twenties. They both were slender, and had long, blond hair."

"But," said Julie, "it's possible the same man's responsible."

"True. But Waco police have contacted us. They had a similar case last autumn, unsolved. Same sort of victim. Young, slim, blond."

"Well, you can't dismiss Rebecca just because she wasn't young or slim or blond," Julie objected. "She's a human being, too. Her life's as important as anybody's."

"We know," Martinez said. "But there's another reason we're reluctant to include your aunt with these other women."

"Yes?" Julie said, challenge in her voice.

Martinez's expression didn't change an iota. "They were hookers. Prostitutes."

"Oh," Julie said, and felt as if she'd shrunk several sizes.

"In addition," Martinez said, "in all three cases, the bodies were dumped in a public place where they'd be easily found. In a city park. Near water."

"Oh," she said again.

"That's confidential," Martinez said. "We don't tell the media everything. It's against our interests. I hope you understand."

Julie nodded. "I understand."

Beside her, Jake stirred restlessly. "Paco, you've run checks on Rebecca Albert. Did you find anything that seemed out of the ordinary?"

Martinez didn't answer immediately. He gave Julie a long look, as if measuring her. At last he said, "Are you aware your aunt lost a lot of money recently? Apparently through bad investments?"

Julie was startled. "Investments? Rebecca?"

Martinez nodded and opened the folder before him. He riffled through it and withdrew a photocopied sheet. "This is from the Casino branch of the Lundeen bank. Last autumn your aunt wrote three large checks. In September, October and November. Five thousand dollars each time."

"Fifteen thousand dollars?" Julie said in disbelief. "That was probably most of her savings."

"It was a good part of it. Her withdrawals left just under six thousand dollars in the account."

She and Jake exchanged questioning glances.

"How do you know it was investments?" Jake asked, one dark eyebrow arching.

"Casino's a little town," Martinez said. "The branch bank is a small one. For her to write three checks like that was unusual. It was remembered."

"Just what were these investments?" asked Jake.

"In oil and gas," Martinez replied. "She mentioned it to one of the tellers. This teller was concerned. Her name is Murray. She told Rebecca to be careful. Rebecca assured her she was working through someone very trustworthy."

Julie frowned skeptically. "Just who was this 'very trustworthy' person?"

"Miss Murray couldn't say. But she remembered the company that the checks were made out to. Norcross and Associates. Later, Rebecca told Murray that she wished she'd taken the teller's advice. She'd no sooner invested than the company went broke. The stock wasn't worth the paper it was printed on."

"Sounds like she might have been scammed," Jake said.

"Well, there you are," Julie said to Martinez, her excitement rising. "There's the lead you've been looking for. What is this—this Norcross and Associates? And who talked Rebecca into investing with them?"

"We can't find them," Martinez said. "I think it was some sort of phantom company, a front. Jake's right. She may have been bilked."

"You can't find them?" she asked, appalled. "You should be leaving no stone unturned—this might be why she disappeared. Maybe she knew too much about this outfit, and they wanted to keep her quiet."

Martinez looked unimpressed. "It's a long shot, Miss FitzJames. But we'll keep it in mind."

"Maybe the man with the turquoise rings was connected with the phoney investment company somehow," she persisted. "Maybe he arranged to meet her because she was threatening to expose them. Then he spirited her off and did God knows what to her."

Martinez eyed her, his expression unreadable.

"And why haven't you found this man with the rings yet?" she asked. "He's the key to the whole thing. Where have you looked? How *hard* have you looked?"

"Julie," Jake said, a warning in his voice.

"We're still checking it out," Martinez said, his gaze holding hers.

"How? When? How often? Every day? How many people are looking? Where are they looking?"

"We're doing everything we can," Martinez said with his maddening calm.

"Then do more," Julie said. "I'm a taxpayer. You're a detective— Do some detecting, dammit."

"I've told you all I can," said Martinez. "I'm sorry."

Jake stood. "Come on, Julie. We can't do any more here."

He took her by the arm, and drew her to her feet.

"Thanks, Paco," Jake said. "She's upset. You know how it goes."

"Yeah," said Martinez. "I know. Good to see you, Jake. Miss FitzJames, we'll keep you informed."

"Do not," Julie said, stabbing her finger toward Martinez, "turn your backs on this case. Do not sweep it under the rug. I want my aunt *found*. And I'll keep after you until it's done."

"She's very grateful to you in her way," Jake told the detective wryly. He maneuvered Julie out the door, closed it behind him and put on his Stetson, pulling it down to its usual angle.

"I'm not grateful," she fumed. "Don't joke about it. It isn't funny."

"I know it's not. I've sat in that same hot seat he was in, myself. The I'm-a-taxpayer speech means the conversation's gone too far. Come on."

"Where are we going?" she asked. He had her by the arm, and she tried, unsuccessfully, to twist away. He didn't release her.

"We're going to Casino to check things out. But first we're going to an ice-cream parlor."

"An ice-cream parlor? Why?"

"To cool you off. And to get you to eat something. I've never known you to turn down a banana split."

"Don't patronize me. I don't want ice cream. The thought of it disgusts me."

"Then we'll go somewhere else, and by God you will eat. You wouldn't last night, you wouldn't this morning, and I didn't come from Tulsa to watch you turn anorexic."

"All right, all right, I'll eat," she said as they left the station and reached the sun-drenched sidewalk. "Just let go, will you?"

He released her, and she brushed her arm as if to remove any memory of his touch. But where his hand had gripped her, her flesh tingled in a pleasant and forbiddenly exciting way.

Suddenly Jake gave a sardonic laugh.

She slid him a sideways look. "What's so funny?"

"If that office had crammed us any closer together," he said with a wicked smile, "you might be carrying my child by now."

JAKE PICKED the nearest restaurant, even though it was a brand-new one that radiated blandness. Its exterior was imitation southwestern and as clean as a whistle.

"Look," he said. "I never saw faux adobe before. Made out of the finest materials to resemble mud. Ingenious."

The interior was as spotless as the outside. On one wall an unimaginative mural had been painted: a Mexican man sat leaning against a wall, his sombrero hiding his face; stylized cacti rose from the dunes of a stylized desert and a stylized coyote with a kerchief round its neck howled at a stylized sky.

Jake led her to a table with a blinding-white cloth and a potted plastic cactus. He asked the waitress to bring them two beers. A moment later, the woman brought them frosted mugs and two bottles garnished with lime wedges.

Jake poured their drinks, then clinked his mug against hers. "To Austin's finest," he said. "Martinez is right. The department's doing all it can."

She shot him a glance of smoldering disappointment. "You don't have to tell me that. The police keep saying it—ad nauseam. If they have no leads after a couple of weeks, they shove the case into the file-and-forget drawer. Well, I won't forget. And I won't let them forget, either."

He picked up a menu and handed it to her. He knew her resentment was born of love, not orneriness. She was stubborn and idealistic and didn't have a drop of quitter's blood in her veins. But while he admired her tenacity, he knew it would probably bring her only heartache.

"Julie," he said, "I don't like to say this, but—"

"But you'll say it anyway."

"Yes. The police are overworked, underpaid and there aren't enough hours in the day for them to do what they're supposed to. A case like Rebecca's, it gets pushed back because there's no proof of foul play. They haven't one clue that says something bad happened to her."

"So nobody gets too concerned," Julie said, her eyes flashing, "until the day somebody finds a body that turns out to be hers. It might be in ten days. It might be in ten years. But then, they'll say, 'Gee, we should have been looking for this woman.'"

He took a deep breath, then released it. "That's exactly right. I'm sorry, but it is."

"Do you know what the police remind me of?" she said, gripping the edge of the table. "Ostriches, that's what. There's a problem here, but they hide their heads in the sand and pretend it doesn't exist. I can't stand by and see nothing being done. It's not right."

He could see her turmoil, her torment. "I'll do what I can," he promised. "I'll stay as long as I can."

She looked at him, some of the fight going out of her eyes. For a moment, she looked almost beseeching, like a a wistful little girl. "How long *can* you stay, Jake? A week, like you said?"

On the phone he'd told her a week. It was a ridiculously short time for a problem as complex as a disappearance. He wondered if she knew that.

"I can stay two if you need me," he said. "I'll stay as long as I can."

She gave him a small smile. It was worth coming five hundred miles to see, he thought, his heart doing a kickstep in his chest.

"You're a good guy, Jake," she said. "And a good cop. I'm glad you're here."

He shook his head. "A better cop than a man, maybe. That's how I lost you. You're my missing person. Do you suppose I'll **ever** find you again?"

She smiled again but shook her head. "Let's not talk about the past. Besides, you don't mean that. I think you throw off sweet talk the way a flower does perfume. You can't help it."

He said nothing. He figured the smartest thing for a man justly accused of sweet talk was to shut up.

She looked at her bottle of beer. With one stroke of her thumbnail, she slit its label down the middle.

She looked up at him, a hint of the old mischief in her eyes. "You know what we used to say when we were stupid kids in college, Jake? That if a girl could rip that whole label through with one motion, she was a virgin. That was the irrefutable proof."

"But you're not a virgin," he said. "I'm delighted to know that for a fact."

She laughed softly, but sadness played in her smile. "It was just a silly thing we said. Virgins. The vanishing breed, excuse the pun. You know, I think Rebecca was a virgin. That's sad, isn't it?"

Jake shrugged. "Maybe she liked it that way. Some do."

"Maybe she did. But if she did, and somebody did something vile to her—violated her in some horrible way, I'll—"

"Shh," he soothed. "Don't." He took her hand, held it tight to reassure her. He was surprised she let him, but she did. She acted as if she hardly noticed.

"Now I wish Rebecca had had a lover—just one, but one who'd made her happy. Life didn't give her much. Everything passed her by. She always lived at the edge of things, like a churchmouse, grateful for the few crumbs she got. I hate it."

"Julie, don't grieve yet. You don't know that life has passed her by. For all we know, she's in Monte Carlo with her hair bleached blond and a twenty-year-old gigolo waiting on her hand and foot, bringing her champagne."

She gave him a resentful look, pulled her hand free of his. "Haven't you listened to one thing I said? Nothing points to her going away voluntarily—not one thing."

Jake was trained to look at all the angles, and did. "You called her a creature of habit. Your creature of habit was about to buy a new car and get a new dog. She changed a flattering hairdo for a frumpy one. She lost fifteen thousand bucks gambling on oil wells, and she was drinking in public with a man nobody can identify. Does this sound like a routine to you?"

"How typical," Julie countered. "Blame the victim. It's like saying a woman asked to be raped. I forgot what a male chauvinist you are."

At that moment, the waitress reappeared, full of smiles and perkiness. "Can I take your order? Or do you need more time?"

Julie pushed away her menu with aversion. "I'm not hungry."

"Order something," Jake said grimly. "Or I'll catch the next plane back to Tulsa. And you can chase your aunt and starve by yourself."

She glared and tried to stare him down. She should have known it wouldn't have worked—how had she forgotten?

She sighed in disdain and said to the waitress, "I'll have a salad and the gazpacho."

"That's hardly enough to keep a bird alive," Jake muttered.

"It's what I want."

Jake shook his head, then turned to the waitress. "Bring me the chili rellenos, the beef fajitas and another beer," he told the woman.

"You betcha," she said brightly, jotting down his order. She flashed another smile and hurried off, oblivious of the tension at their table.

"I also forgot," Julie said tightly, "how high-handed you are. I do not need to be told to eat."

"And I forgot how hardheaded you are," he countered. "Skip a few more meals, and you'll fall over. That's really bright, Julie. That's good thinking."

She stared past him, as if she were looking at a vision that sapped her anger and sobered her. "Let's not fight, Jake," she said quietly, facing him again. "We did enough of that in the past."

"Yeah," he said. "We did."

"All I want," she said, "is to find Rebecca. I'm scared. I'm really scared, and I'm not used to that feeling. Does that make sense?"

It made perfect sense. Fear was a foreign emotion to her. And perhaps never before in her brave, headlong life had Julie ever felt helpless.

"I'm sorry." He said it mechanically, but he felt it deeply. He hated seeing her pain.

She hadn't so much as sipped her beer. But she took the bottle in her hand and gazed at the label slit in half by her thumbnail.

Virginity, Jake thought darkly. *I'm here to find a fifty-year-old virgin who's never surprised anybody in her life. Until now.*

"I really do wish she'd had at least one love affair," Julie said. "A wonderful one. So she'd have had some sweetness, some tenderness, some warmth to remember fondly when the winter nights stretched out dark and cold."

He injected mockery into his voice, although he felt none. "Is that how you remember me? Fondly? Sweetly? Warmly?"

She gave him one of those deadly honest looks that only she could give, the sort that shook his soul. She said, "It hurts too much to remember you. So I try not to do it at all."

Oh, Julie, he wanted to say, *I have loved you so much it's nearly killed me. It's worse than death could ever be. I would sell my soul to be in bed with you again, to love every sweet inch of your body. To be naked with you, to be inside you, you on the top and me on the bottom. To hold your waist as you bend above me, your hair like a silken tent about us, while we come together.*

I would gladly die for that.

Gladly. Gladly.

Instead, he looked at the mural and said, "That is the damnedest most stupid-looking coyote I ever saw."

4

JULIE DROVE BACK to the hotel, Jake silent beside her. During lunch, he'd said something sarcastic about the coyote painted on the wall, then he'd gone broody on her.

Moody silence was not his style. He was not an extremely talkative man, but he had a sardonic, easy charm and was seldom at a loss for words.

Troubled, she wondered if he wished he hadn't come. Maybe he'd decided that he didn't want her, after all, that she wasn't worth the trouble. The thought shook her with painful force, even though she'd told herself a thousand times that she would never take him back. Never.

The heart is a hive of crazy bees;
Their honey, their honey will give you no ease.

The lines of poetry came to her unbidden. She could not even remember where she'd read them. But at the moment, they seemed all too accurate.

She pulled up in the hotel parking lot. "You're awfully quiet," she said, feeling defensive.

"So are you," he said, tugging down his Stetson to a wicked angle. "What are you thinking about?"

"Bees," she said vaguely. "What were you thinking about?"

The corner of his mouth flicked upward in the old, familiar smile. "Birds," he said, giving her a sideways glance. "Maybe we could get together. The birds and the bees."

Her emotions buzzed more crazily, but she tried to give him a stern look. "Don't flirt. Do you really want to check out of here and go clear to Casino?"

He eyed her lazily. "Yes. And if my baggage hasn't caught up with me, you can buy me a fresh shirt and underwear."

"You don't wear underwear," she said without thinking, then felt her face go hot with embarrassment.

"Ah," he said, "you remember."

She remembered all too well, of course. He never wore T-shirts or briefs. If they'd started kissing and caressing while they were fully clothed, she never had to grope through layers of clothing to touch his skin.

A few shirt buttons undone, and his chest was bare, hard and bronzed before her, ready for her to lay her cheek against it, press her lips to it. A snap and a tug at a zipper, and the thick, upright stalk of his manhood was there, brushing her fingertips.

Unlike him, she always seemed bound up in layer after layer of coverings: once it had been a linen jacket over a crocheted vest over a turtleneck over a slip over a bra—in mock frustration he had growled against her neck, "Dammit, I know you're in there somewhere."

She looked away from him, the blood heating her cheeks even more shamefully. He kept his body free, his emotions bound and hidden. She bound and hid her body, but her feelings were too often exposed and naked. He and she were too different, always had been, always would be.

"Julie," he said quietly, "you look unhappy. What's wrong? I didn't mean to make you unhappy."

"It's nothing," she lied. "I'm fine. Let's check out."

The heart is a hive of crazy bees;
Their honey, their honey will give you no ease.

"I'd give a lot," he said in the same low voice, "to know what's going through your head right now."

"I'm thinking of bees," she snapped, knowing the answer was ridiculous. "And how much I hate honey."

For a moment she thought he was about to touch her, and if he did, she didn't know what would happen. But he made no move toward her. "You don't hate honey," he said. "You used to love it."

"I don't," she insisted with a shake of her head. She raised her chin and gave him a resentful look. "Honey's terrible stuff. Bees spit it out, then walk around in it with their naked little bug feet. It's disgusting."

He got out of the car, walked to her side and opened her door. He offered her his hand. "It's sweet and it's natural," he said, and she knew he was talking not about honey, but about sex.

She ignored his hand, she refused to reply. She got out by herself, careful not to even so much as brush near him. "Let's get out of this place," she said.

THE DESK CLERK, a stout, middle-aged man with a low forehead and a high voice, was snippy about their checking out late. "The time is clearly posted," he said. "This is highly irregular," he said. "I *should* hold you responsible for another day's stay. This throws everything off schedule—"

Jake flashed his badge. "This concerns police business. This hotel is implicated, we'll see how deeply. Now, the bill."

The patches on the clerk's mottled face flushed more deeply and spread. He pressed his lips together and tapped furiously at his computer keyboard. He handed over the bill, and when he spoke, his voice had gone even higher, "Just sign here, please."

He looked on disapprovingly as Julie signed. Then he glared even more disapprovingly at Jake, as if to say, "Does police business always have you staying in hotels with a beautiful woman, where *she* signs for the charges?"

Jake gave him his Grade C intimidating stare. It worked like a charm. The man dropped his gaze, his complexion developed even larger and pinker splotches and he did not meet Jake's eyes again or so much as glance at Julie.

"Come on," Jake said to her, slinging his suitbag over his shoulder. "Let's go."

His luggage, a suitbag and a duffel bag, had finally arrived. Julie refused to let him carry her suitcase for her. It was a large, battered soft-sided suitcase, its gray nylon scuffed and stained from years of use. He remembered it well.

With a pang, he recalled he'd intended to buy her new luggage as part of her wedding present. Good quality, not this cheap, discount-store stuff. He'd meant to have her new initials put on it—J.G., for Julie Good Thunder.

Dream on, he told himself bitterly, and wondered, not for the first time, if there was now someone else in her life, a man who wanted to change her initials to his.

In the parking lot, he opened the trunk of her car. The trunk was messy, as always, he noted, shaking his head. Before he could pack in their luggage, he had to move the spare tire, a collapsible easel and a stuffed armadillo.

Finally, he eased the lid shut. "Do you mind me asking why you have a dead armadillo in your trunk?"

She shook her head so that her long dark hair swung like a silken cape. "It would be cruel to have a live one in there, wouldn't it?"

He sighed harshly and opened the door on the driver's side for her. "Let me rephrase that. Why do you have an armadillo in your trunk at all?"

He paced to the other side, then slid into the passenger seat. "Well?" he said, looking at her beautiful profile.

"I had a commission," she told him as she pulled out of her parking space. "To paint an armadillo by some wild azaleas. Live ones hate posing. Dead ones don't mind as much."

"I don't imagine so. Did you stuff it yourself?"

She shot him a superior glance then turned her attention back to the traffic. Did he only imagine he saw a glint of amusement in her eyes? Or was it really there? He hoped so.

"A taxidermist gave it to me," she told him.

Jake had a dark vision of an amorous taxidermist wooing Julie with dead wildlife, and he didn't like it. "It's only got three legs," he said. "The armadillo. I call that a lousy gift."

A strained patience came into her voice. "That's *why* old Mr. Gabbard gave it to me. It's now my very own personal armadillo, so please don't criticize it."

Old Mr. Gabbard, he reflected. A man who gave away only incomplete animals. That didn't sound so threatening.

He decided to tease her, as he had in the old days. "So how do you explain it? Why the armadillo in your picture has only three legs?"

"He doesn't," she said with even more exaggerated patience. "The armadillo in the picture has four legs."

"How's that possible?"

Her nose went up a bit more haughtily. "I *imagine* the fourth leg."

"Why don't you just imagine the whole armadillo? Saves on trunk space."

She laughed. It was a small laugh, more exasperation than mirth, but it did his heart good to hear it again after all this time.

The laugh died all too quickly, and her face went serious, almost sad. "I shouldn't be joking around," she said. "And we don't need to be talking armadillos. We need to talk about Rebecca."

He paused a moment, studying her now-solemn profile, the way her hair cascaded down in smooth dark waves so that it actually touched the car seat. He wished he could reach over, touch the corner of her mouth, gently guide it into smiling again.

Feeling more solemn himself, he said, "Julie, just because Rebecca's gone doesn't mean it's wrong for you ever to smile or laugh again. You know that, don't you?"

She nodded but said nothing.

"No matter what's happened, sooner or later you've got to get on with your own life."

He hesitated again, knowing what he was about to add was the most painful fact she could be forced to face. "You may never find out what's become of her. If that happens, you have to accept it and go on. Live, laugh, smile. Your smile's too beautiful for the world to lose."

He saw the sudden glint of tears in her eyes and knew he'd gone too far. She blinked them back angrily, as if grief was a weakness that offended her.

She kept her eyes trained on the road like a soldier on watch. "Don't talk about my smile. Talk about my aunt. What are we going to do in Casino?"

"Talk to people that knew her," he said.

"The police have already done that. They found nothing. Everybody's as puzzled and shocked as I am."

"We'll talk to them again. And I want to see her house. Can you still get into it?"

"Yes," she said. "I've got a key. It's not cordoned off with yellow tape, like it's a crime scene or something. The police have been through it."

She blinked back her tears again, then took a deep breath. "Like I told you, I'd been through it, too. Right before I reported her missing. That's the only thing in her house that the police found out of the ordinary. *My* fingerprints."

"We'll look again. And Julie?"

"Yes?"

"How does the rest of your family feel about the situation?"

They were heading out of Austin now, leaving the peculiar geometry of its skyline behind. She seemed to search for words. "Rebecca's family is small. The others are disturbed—concerned. But—it's not like they were close to her. They weren't."

He sank more deeply against the seat, trying to relax. It was tempting to rest his left arm on the armrest between them, furtively let the ebony spill of her hair touch him. He set his teeth, crossed his arms and settled in for the long drive ahead.

"So tell me," he said. "About your family. You never said much about them."

Except, he thought, *I always got the hint they wouldn't approve of me. And maybe they didn't quite approve of you, either, sugar.*

JULIE ALWAYS FOUND it difficult to talk intimately about her family, precisely because it was a family in which little intimacy existed.

It wasn't that she didn't love them; she did. But they were a group of highly independent and quirky people, with Julie perhaps the most independent and quirky of all.

Her father and mother and two brothers were practical people who valued stability, hard facts and cold common sense. Julie was the lone romantic spirit.

From the corner of her eye, she could see Jake, lounging against the seat, his arms crossed with maddening casualness. He was a man of action and hard facts. Could he understand the peculiar web of subtleties that bound the women of her family?

She switched on the casette player so that her favorite tape could give her emotional support, and the lead singer's voice filled the car.

She squared her jaw. "All right," she said. "But it gets all tangled. First, Rebecca isn't my aunt completely. I suppose she's my half aunt. I don't know how to put it exactly."

"Put it however you can," Jake said. "Take your time. It's a long way to Casino."

She took a deep breath, her fingers tightening on the wheel. "All right. My grandmother's name was Frances. She had two daughters. The older one is my mother, Lynn. The younger one is Rebecca. But Frances was married twice. Lynn and Rebecca had different fathers."

"Okay," he said. "I can comprehend that. Frances married twice. It's practically un-American not to."

Julie ignored his cynicism. "My grandfather's name was Hank. He died young, of a massive heart attack, in 1943. Lynn was twelve years old. My grandmother married again, within the year. A man named Will Albert. Lynn never accepted Will. And she never really forgave my grandmother for marrying him."

She felt him give her a curious look that sent a frisson of awareness scuttling through her nerve endings. He said, "Do you always call your mother Lynn?"

She stared at the road, and nodded. "Yes. From the time I was twelve. It's how it was done in our family. My older brothers teased me for using Mama. They said it showed I was a baby. I couldn't wait to start calling my parents Lynn and Clark instead of Mom and Dad."

He shifted his weight slightly, recrossing his long legs. She could still feel his eyes on her. "You never told me that before."

She frowned slightly. "I've always found it hard to explain. Besides, you and I never really did much talking. Except when we fought."

"That's not true, and you know it. You just never talked about your family, and I didn't push you. I figured you would tell me when you felt ready."

For the second time since they'd left Austin, Julie felt the absurd and painful desire to cry. When she'd been with Jake, her world revolved around him. She hadn't wanted to speak of her family because they were *different*, and her memories of them were puzzling and somehow painful.

Well, she thought, the time had come to talk about them at last. "Lynn—my mother—hated it that my grandmother remarried. And then, the next year, there was a new baby to deal with, as well."

"Rebecca," Jake said.

"Rebecca," she agreed. "But there was a fourteen-year age difference between Lynn and Rebecca. And four years later, Lynn left for college. That's all the time they lived together—four years. When Lynn left home, Rebecca wasn't even in kindergarten yet."

"So they were never close," Jake said. It was a statement, not a question.

"No," Julie answered. "But Lynn was always *concerned* about Rebecca. And Rebecca absolutely idolized her—she thought Lynn was an angel and a beauty queen and a Hollywood star all rolled into one."

"Your mother is beautiful?" he asked.

"She's incredibly beautiful," Julie said honestly. "She probably *could* have been a Hollywood star if she'd wanted."

"So that's where you get your looks," he said. "I should have known. Movie-star genes."

She darted him a disdainful glance. He always went on and on about her appearance, which was nothing special when compared to her mother's. Once, his flattery had swept her away. Even now it had its allure, and she had to remind herself to beware of it. She had no special cause for vanity.

She turned her attention back to the highway. A coyote streaked in front of her car, a bolt of ragtag fur, and she slowed to give the animal a margin of safety.

"My mother married right out of college," she continued. "She had a teaching degree, but she never used it. She and Clark—my father—had two sons, my big brothers. She stayed in touch with my grandmother and with Rebecca. But she wouldn't have anything to do with Will Albert. She couldn't stand him. And Rebecca went on thinking that Lynn hung the moon. She'd visit every time Lynn let her."

"Lynn would 'let' her visit?" Jake asked, too quickly for comfort. "You make it sound as if Lynn was granting her some royal privilege."

That's exactly how Julie suspected it was, and felt critical and disloyal for thinking it. But Lynn had always acted as if there was an innate inequality between herself and her half sister. Being Hank's beautiful daughter made Lynn a princess in her own mind. And being Will's plain daughter made Rebecca seem a commoner. None of this was ever spoken aloud. But Julie was certain that she, Lynn and Rebecca all understood this perception.

"Oh, Lynn always said she and Rebecca didn't have much in common, that's all," Julie said, wishing she didn't feel so uncomfortable.

It suddenly occurred to her that maybe she hadn't told Jake about her family, not because he wouldn't understand, but because he would understand too well—better than she, herself, wanted to, perhaps.

"Lynn had a lot of obligations," she said in defense of her mother. "A big house to take care of. Two boys to raise. And my father had a lot of social obligations."

"Your father's a bank vice president, right?"

"Right," she said. She remembered telling Jake her father was a banker, and how Jake had ever after teased her that he was after her family money, not her.

"So your daddy's rich, and your mama's good-looking," he said sardonically. "Just like the song says. Was Rebecca jealous?"

"My father's well-to-do," Julie said firmly. "But he's not rich. Not by a long shot. And Rebecca wasn't jealous. She didn't have a jealous bone in her body. She adored my mother. She went to college and got a teaching degree. I don't think it was because she wanted to teach—she just wanted to be like her big sister."

"But she wasn't like her big sister," Jake said. "Not in any way, to judge from her photo. She never had a family of her own, a husband, a lover, not even a boyfriend?"

The thought saddened Julie. "Not that I know of. After my grandmother died, she only had her father, Will Albert. And he *was* a nasty man. Bossy and critical and manipulative. I met him a few times."

"What happened to Frances?" Jake asked. "Your grandmother?"

"She died two years before I was born. The same year Rebecca graduated from college. I guess Rebecca was very shaken. All she had left was Will. She went home to Casino, taught there and lived in the house. Teaching was actually her second job. Taking care of him was her first priority—at least in his eyes."

"So by the time you were born, Rebecca was on her way to being the classic spinster schoolteacher?"

"I'm afraid so," Julie said. "She'd come for short visits during school vacations. Just a day or so. And she'd always bring presents for us. Too many presents, my mother said."

Jake said, "Did she want to come for long visits? Not just short ones?"

Julie had hoped he wouldn't ask that question. It was one she'd asked herself too many times, and she didn't like the answer. "I suppose she did. But Lynn was still always so busy. And to be frank, she didn't completely respect Rebecca. She said that Rebecca let Will run her life. That she had no gumption, no backbone. She didn't say that to her face, of course."

Jake was silent for the next few miles, as if mulling over what she'd told him. "So this Will Albert and your family were the only relatives Rebecca had?" he said finally.

"Yes. My father has a big family. I've got seven aunts and uncles on his side, and about twenty cousins. But on Lynn's side, there was only Rebecca."

"And Will Albert died, I take it?" Jake asked.

Damn, damn, thought Julie. *I don't want to tell him this part. But I should. I have to.*

She gave one grim nod. "He died. Four years ago. And that's when Lynn and Rebecca had their—their falling-out."

At the edge of her vision, she saw Jake turn his face toward her. "A falling-out? When old Will died? What about? Property of some kind, I'll bet."

She gripped the steering wheel still more tightly and thought, with chagrin, that he was too good at zeroing in on these things. "The house," she admitted. "My mother wanted the house she'd grown up in. Her father had built it. She thought it should be at least half hers."

"But it wasn't," Jake said. "When Frances died, she left it to Will, and when Will died, he left it to Rebecca, his only daughter. And not one thing to your mother, right? And she was—excuse my French—royally pissed off."

Julie's shoulders sagged in embarrassed acknowledgment. As inelegant as Jake's description was, it was accurate. Lynn's anger had shown itself as hauteur, but the hauteur had been so cold, it was awesome.

She made a helpless, one-handed gesture. "Look, Jake, I love my mother. But I have to admit, she acted badly over this. The law's the law. I don't know why she ever expected the house to be left to her even in part, but she did. It's because her father had built it, I guess. She had no reason to be affronted or disappointed, but she was. She's hardly spoken to Rebecca since Will's death."

Jake shifted again. He was such a tall man, he must be uncomfortable in her little car. She stole a glance at him. His dark eyes were on her face, and she thought she saw hunger in them, hunger for her.

Quickly she looked away, because an exciting, forbidden fluttering was filling her midsection.

"It's nothing to be ashamed of," he said, his voice low.

For a giddy moment, she thought he meant the chemistry between them. She could think of no answer and her breath stuck in her throat.

But he was speaking of something else. "These family quarrels—they happen," he said. "Yours isn't the first, it won't be the last."

She swallowed, unable to meet his gaze, which she knew was trained on her. "I know my family isn't the first or the last," she said. "I just hoped they'd be *better.* I was disappointed. I was glad I'd finished college and didn't have to go home anymore."

"Wait a minute," Jake said. "What do you mean? You haven't been home since this trouble about the house?"

Julie squirmed slightly in her seat. "Of course I go home, just not often. A few days at Christmas, Easter, Thanksgiving. I call once a month—you know that."

"Yeah," he said. "I remember that. Sure. I remember."

During her weeks of living with Jake, she'd called home at 1:00 p.m. on the first Sunday of each month. She'd chat the first twenty minutes with her mother, then five with her father, who never had much to say, then five more with her mother.

They discussed family matters. How were her parents? How were her brothers? Her brothers' wives? How was her father's business? Her mother's clubs and luncheons and parties? How was Julie's career going? It was not a cold conversation, but it was never warm, and it followed the same pattern, call after call.

When Julie moved to Oklahoma City with Jake, she told her mother she was moving because she'd found someone she was seriously interested in. She didn't bother to tell her father; he did not discuss such matters and preferred to hear them from her mother.

Lynn had seemed only mildly curious about Julie's new relationship, nothing more. Julie was not surprised; she knew her mother's aloofness all too well.

After Julie and Jake broke up, and Julie moved back to her little house in the hill country, she'd had to admit to her mother her "serious" romance was over. All Lynn had said was, "What's to be, will be." Julie had feared her parents might disapprove of Jake because of his Native American blood, but suspected Lynn would never admit to such a thing.

As if Jake could read her mind, he said, "Your folks didn't like you being mixed up with the likes of me, did they?"

Her muscles, already stiff with stress, tensed even more. She realized her whole body ached from the anxiety of having Jake so near again.

"I don't know," she said without emotion. "They didn't say much."

"And what," he challenged, "do they think of you going off with me like this to look for Rebecca?"

She glanced at the countryside, which was growing flatter, the hills falling away into a more barren and dusty landscape.

"They don't know I'm looking for Rebecca, and they don't know I called you. I'm an adult. I don't report my every move to them. They don't expect me to."

"I see," he said. "Your own woman. As always. So they didn't influence your decision to walk out on me. Or maybe, deep down, they did."

She saw a rest stop ahead and decided to pull over.

"Jake, I don't want to talk about you and me. There's nothing more to say. I've got to stop and stretch. And take an aspirin. My head's starting to ache."

She pulled off the road and parked in the shade of a live oak, from which a blue jay cried harshly. Without speaking she got out of the car and went to the picnic table in a small stand of mesquite trees. No one else was at the rest stop.

She braced her arms against the tabletop and stretched, standing on tiptoe and arching her back like a cat. She heard Jake slam the car door. She sensed that he had drawn near and stopped behind her, so close she could feel his presence.

She didn't turn around, but lowered her heels to the ground, stopped stretching and stayed leaning against the table. She gazed, unseeing, at the horizon of the rolling plain. Her hair spilled down on either side of her face like a black curtain, and she was glad it covered her face. It made her feel somehow hidden, safe.

But there was no hiding from Jake. He sat on the tabletop, almost lazily, and said, "Push that mane back so I can see you, will you? Would you look me in the eye? You haven't done it for about a hundred and fifty miles."

Impatiently, she pushed her hair over her shoulder so it hung down her back, and forced herself to look into his long-lashed black eyes.

"Okay," he said. "I've got no right to keep asking about you and me. That's not why I'm here. But tell me one more thing about your family."

Warily, she stared at him. She had once loved his face, even though she could seldom read it. She could not read it now.

"I have a feeling there's something missing. Let's go over it again. How exactly have your family reacted to Rebecca's disappearance?"

She straightened up from the table and crossed her arms, as if she felt a sudden chill. "They're concerned, of course," she said. "But . . ." Her voice trailed off.

"But what, Julie?" he asked, his voice surprisingly gentle. "You can tell me."

The wind rose, stirring her hair and making the mesquite leaves rustle. "At first they were disturbed. But now they just—accept it. They've taken it in stride. And Lynn . . ."

Again her voice failed her. He bent nearer to her, and for one confusing moment she thought he was going to take her chin in his hand and turn her face to his. But he made no move to touch her.

"And Lynn?" he urged. "Your mother? What about her?"

Julie crossed her arms more tightly. "She's starting to wonder if—"

"Yes?"

She shook her head in a mixture of despair and embarrassment. "She's starting to wonder how soon the house will be hers if Rebecca doesn't come back. Rebecca left her the house in her will, you see. She made sure Lynn knew. She tried to heal the rift that way. Oh, I don't want to talk about it!"

She turned from him and gazed across the highway, past her silver car. The same brownish rolling country filled her vision, stretching on, it seemed, forever.

She was ashamed that her family had recovered so quickly from the shock of Rebecca's disappearance, ashamed that Lynn had so quickly become more concerned about her sister's house than her sister.

"Tell me," she said, raising her chin and watching a hawk wheeling in the wind. "After I left, did you find the person who murdered Billy the Kid?"

She gazed up at the hawk and thought of Billy Cable, so young, handsome, idealistic and eager to serve justice. Jake must have risen from the table and stepped behind her. His voice was in her ear, his breath warm against her flesh.

"What do you think?" he said in a rough whisper.

The hawk soared and dived, then soared again. "I think you did," she said in a tight voice. "Didn't you?"

"Yes," he said. "It was a drug dealer. Not much older than Billy. He's in the state prison. For life. No parole."

She stood straighter, watched the sky harder, but she could no longer see the hawk or even the streaming clouds; her vision was too blurred. She bit her lower lip so hard it hurt. It didn't help.

"Julie?" he said with concern, "are you crying? What made you cry? This business about Rebecca? Or Billy? Or both?"

His hands were on her shoulders now, and at his touch she went weak. "Everything," she said miserably, turning to him.

And by *everything*, she meant not only Rebecca and her own family, and Billy Cable, but Jake and herself, as well. Maybe she meant life itself, which suddenly seemed too complicated and far too cruel.

But although she knew she could never live with Jake, she clung to him as tightly as she could. She laid her face against his chest and wept.

He held her close, as if he never meant to let her go.

5

HE LOWERED his face to hers and kissed her. And it felt right. She was where she had wanted to be from the first time she'd seen him again, in his arms, body to body, his lips upon her own.

A cardinal sang in the mesquite, a distant song she barely heard. The breeze rose, lifting her hair so it fluttered about their joined bodies in dark, waving ribbons. Julie twined her arms around his neck and felt bereft when he took his mouth from hers.

But he held her more tightly still, and he was kissing her tears away and whispering to her, "You were never good at crying. So stop—all right?"

His lips moved gently yet hungrily over her streaked cheeks, her hot eyelids, her fluttering lashes. "Don't cry," he said softly. "I hate it when you're sad."

Then why, she thought, *did you make me sad so often?* But, paradoxically, she was happy to be so close to him again, and sad that she was happy, and too confused to do anything except press against him with the same wild need she felt in his bunched muscles.

His mouth claimed hers once more, and his tongue traced the soft, moist lining of her upper lip, grazing her teeth. She opened her lips more widely, to taste his tongue and invite it more deeply inside her mouth, just as she suddenly craved his body deep within hers, as deep as possible.

She knew he was naked beneath his shirt and jeans, and the knowledge dizzied her with longing. He groaned and put his hand on her buttocks, pulling her closer to him, and she felt as if she was losing control.

But it was broad daylight, and they were in a public place . . .

A car door slammed. And another. Children's shrieks and laughter pierced the air, breaking the soft whisper of the wind.

"Look—they're tradin' spit!"

A disgruntled adult female voice broke into the merriment. "You kids hush up and do your business. Bubba, help your brother sit on the toilet seat and get his pants back up. Nadine, you come with me."

"Mush alert!" a boy cried euphorically, while the others giggled, and then there was the sound of rest room doors opening and shutting.

Jake drew away and stared down at her. "Let's get out of here before Bubba gets his brother's pants back up, what do you say?"

Julie dropped her hands from his neck, swiftly and guiltily, her cheeks flaming. Jake seized her by the hand and led her back to her car.

"You're too tense to drive," he said, opening the door on the passenger's side. "Let me take over for a while."

She didn't object. She got in and glanced at the empty car beside hers. Its back-window shelf was littered with plastic toys and children's books, and a rag doll had been thrown carelessly on the dashboard, its black button eyes shining in the sun.

"I hope," Jake said, getting in and fastening his seat belt, "that when Bubba's old enough to get a girl in a clinch, the yard apes come dancing around him like devils."

She smiled in spite of herself, as he quickly pulled out of the parking lot and sped down the highway. Her head had begun to ache again. She hadn't taken the aspirin; she had indulged in much stronger medicine—desire—and it had left her dazed and feverish.

Why did I let him do that? she asked herself, wondering what Pandora's box she'd opened.

Because you were tired and distraught, her mind answered, and she wanted to believe that age-old and dependable reason.

Because you never stopped missing him, wanting him, her heart, less the hypocrite, protested. But it did not add, *loving him.* She'd known from the time she'd learned that Billy Cable was murdered that she could no longer let herself love Jake. It was too dangerous.

What had happened at the rest stop was as inevitable as it was wrong, she thought. She should have been stronger, should have resisted. But she hadn't, and now the chemistry between her and Jake had changed; it was far more volatile. She hoped it was not symbolic that he, not she, was the one now in the driver's seat.

AFTER THE REST-STOP incident, Jake decided not only did he never want children, he didn't want other people to have them, either. He would be able to do without the evil little imps for the rest of his life.

But what would have happened if the second car had not come along? He had wanted Julie with all his heart, soul and hungry body, and she had acted, for a moment, as if she wanted him, too.

Would he have been so swept away that he would have tried to make love to her in the tussocky brown grass or atop the picnic table? Or, assuming he had enough rational mind left to think of it, in the back seat of her car?

First, she wasn't that kind of girl, and second, the highway patrol could arrest people for that sort of cavorting. But for a moment there, he'd wanted her so much he would have made love to her at high noon in Times Square if she'd said yes, and damn the consequences.

Now she was over there, hugging the passenger door, keeping as far away from him as possible, her face hidden by the thick, shining veil of her hair. She regretted that interlude, he knew.

But for those few brief, clear, fiery moments, she had wanted him; he was sure of it. That meant there was hope, and he could make her want him again. He was—well—almost sure of it.

"What happened back there meant nothing," she said suddenly. "It won't happen again."

"Look," he told her flippantly, "it was just the old stimulus-response at work. You felt bad—stimulus. I held you—response. Just like Pavlov's dog."

"Pavlov's dog?" she asked with such spirit that he had to hide a smile. "I *beg* your pardon."

"And I beg yours," he said smoothly. He had to put her at ease again. He was schooled in deception, and knew what he had to do and how to do it.

"Now, where were we?" he asked, all business again. "I remember. Your mother isn't exactly in deepest mourning since Rebecca disappeared. Lynn and your aunt have been on the outs over the house. Tell me about the house."

She stirred slightly, pressing more firmly against the door. She tried to smooth back her long hair, which had been rumpled by the wind. He had to restrain himself from reaching over and smoothing it himself.

"It's not much of a house," she said. "You saw a picture of the porch—the one where Rebecca's standing by the bird feeder."

"Describe it for me," he said. "Describe the neighborhood, the town."

"I don't know where to start," she said, and he heard the reluctance in her voice.

"Just start," he coaxed.

Come on, sugar, just talk to me. Relax and talk to me. Come to Papa, that's a girl.

JULIE WAS RELIEVED when they reached the town limits of Casino. She hadn't known how to describe Casino in charitable terms to Jake. She could barely describe it in charitable terms to herself.

Casino was one of those dusty little towns that people sang about in country-western songs: the sort of place you longed to leave and only wanted to see in your rearview mirror. It had no beauty, no charm, little history, less wealth, and the countryside surrounding it was dry, barren and almost forbidding.

It was nearly dusk when they reached the main street, which was named, of course, Main Street. There were two small restaurants, both closed. There were also two bars, both open.

A single clothing store stood next to one of the bars, its window dark and its door permanently locked. It had been abandoned for years, and by the light of the street lamp, Julie could see a headless mannequin lying on its back, its stiff arms embracing the empty air.

Next to the clothing store was a barbershop, closed for the night, its red-and-white-striped pole in need of repainting.

There were two bank buildings, a State Farm insurance office, a pharmacist's and a real estate office with its window full of snapshots of property for sale. Flanking the north side of the main block, like guardians, were the offices of two competing law firms, Meister and Meister on the east end, McDougall and Son on the west.

Most of the stores seemed permanently shut down and stood empty, their signs fading. The hardware store, the furniture store, the auto supply shop, the variety store, all were forsaken and had a sad, ghostly air.

Jake whistled between his teeth. "This really is the sort of town where they roll up the sidewalks after dark."

"My mother hated it," Julie admitted. "Maybe it rubbed off on me. I never liked the place. But Rebecca did. To her it was home."

"Home sweet home," Jake said, but he sounded dubious.

"Rebecca was born in that building over there," she said, pointing at a small, undistinguished two-story brick structure. "It used to be the hospital. Now it's the sheriff's office and jail. When they changed it, she started saying she'd been born in jail."

She smiled wanly at the memory of Rebecca's little joke.

Jake said, "We'll talk to the sheriff tomorrow."

Julie's smile died. "I suppose. Listen, I know it's too late to talk to anyone tonight. I'll stay at Rebecca's house, and you can stay at the motel. It's not much, but mice won't scamper over your feet or anything. I'll pay, of course."

"No." He said it with startling finality.

"What do you mean—no?" she demanded. "Of course, I'll pay. That's our agreement."

He stopped the car at the stop sign and didn't move on. He didn't have to. No other traffic was coming.

He said, "I mean, no, you're not staying at Rebecca's. I don't want you touching anything else there. I don't want you sleeping in her bed, using her bathroom, straightening her kitchen. We both stay **at the m**otel."

This sounded like a dangerous idea to Julie, and she didn't like it. "The police have already searched her house."

"But I haven't. That's why you brought me into this. To look the case over for myself."

"I don't want to stay in the same motel as you do," Julie protested. "People here know who I am. They'll talk."

"Hell," he said scornfully, "in a town like this, people will talk if we sleep in the same county. I know small towns. I grew up in one."

She shrugged noncommittally, supposing he was right.

Once her mother had bitterly said that gossip in Casino was like the water and sewage system. It ran beneath the town in a complex network, connecting every household, emptying itself in the common, nasty cistern of the town's undying memory.

The image made her shudder with distaste.

"What's wrong?" he asked. "We spent last night in the same hotel. What's so different about this?"

"Nothing," she said with a sigh. "Stay on this street. It leads to the motel. Or are you going to park at this stop sign?"

"It doesn't look as if anybody'd mind," he said, stepping on the gas. They passed the feed store, the used car dealership, Cleo's Cuty and Beauty Shoppe, the Laundromat, the grocery store, and finally, the Casino Public Elementary School.

Julie stared at the motionless swings, the inert teeter-totters, the empty children's slide and deserted jungle gym. For twenty-eight years, Rebecca had taught in this building, monitored this playground.

For over a generation, she had been one of the keepers of the town's children, and the children had been her life. Nothing could have induced her to leave this school, its ties and memories. Julie was certain of that, as certain as if an angel had engraved it in stone.

"Rebecca's school, I take it?" Jake said.

Irreverence edged his voice, and that edge helped her keep a grip on her emotions. She would not cry in front of him again. He was right; the tears had been like an invitation—help me, hold me, kiss me, comfort me. She would not issue the invitation again.

"Yes," she said with a curt nod. "And over there, her church." The First Methodist Church was the second largest of Casino's five churches. The largest was the Baptist, and the smallest was the Catholic.

"She was a Methodist?"

"Lifelong," Julie said. "Next to the school, church was the most important thing in her life. She was in the choir, the ladies' auxiliary, and she taught Sunday school. Her house is just down the next block, around the corner. She spent most of her life in this three-block radius."

"How about we take a look at the house. We won't go in. I just want to see it."

Julie nodded. "Turn right at the stop sign. Down Maple Street."

There were no maples on Maple Street. There were a few scraggly mesquites, evergreen sumacs and horsebean shrubs. The street was quiet, but the lights of a few homes gleamed in the swiftly falling dusk.

Julie pointed to a small, darkened house on the corner. "There," she said, her throat tightening. "Rebecca's house."

Jake slowed, then stopped before it, and in silence the two of them stared at the boxy white house. It had an air of gravelike quiet that made the knot in Julie's throat grow more painful.

"You're right," he said in a low voice. "It doesn't seem like much to fight over, does it?"

"No," Julie whispered, almost to herself. "It doesn't."

The corner lot was a large one, and the small house was the oldest on the block. Its white clapboard exterior needed paint. Its only attractive feature was the front porch, which ran across the whole front of the house. Square white wooden columns supported the porch roof, and the columns were entwined with dead vines that spring had not yet revived.

"The neighborhood seems to be dying," Jake said, nodding in the direction of the houses they'd passed. Of the five on Rebecca's side of the street, two had For Sale signs, as did three on the other side.

"The whole town's dying," Julie said. "All that kept it going was oil and cattle. Now, the oil's played out, and the cattle market's down."

Jake shook his head. "I wonder if she just up and left. I wouldn't want to grow old in a town like this. No, ma'am."

Julie turned to him, fighting down a surge of anger. "Now you sound like everybody else," she said. "Maybe you wouldn't want to live here, and maybe I wouldn't either, but we don't see it through Rebecca's eyes," she said. "There's no place like your own home."

"Isn't there?" he asked, cocking his dark head in that challenging way he had. "You didn't stay in yours, did you? And I didn't stay in mine."

"That's different," she argued. "You're a—an adventurous spirit."

"And you're a free one," he said. "You're saying she was neither? Not adventurous or free?"

"Jake," she said, "please don't do this to me. Rebecca's a homebody. She never left Casino except to go to college."

"The way you talk, I'm surprised she did *that*. Where'd she go?"

"University of Texas of the Permian Basin. At Odessa. The same as Mama—I mean, Lynn."

He gave her a long look, his eyes hidden by the falling shadows. "You called her Mama, all of a sudden. Interesting. Why?"

She sighed with impatience and gazed at the house again. "I don't know why. Because I'm tired and this house reminds me of being little again. What does it matter? What's important is finding Rebecca, not what I call my mother."

"What's important is understanding Rebecca," he corrected. "She and your mother were at odds over this house. What did your mother want with it? Surely to God she didn't expect to retire here or something?"

Julie shrugged and looked at the house, now bluish in the rising moonlight. Such a simple, nondescript bungalow—how had it caused such trouble?

"I told you," she said, keeping her gaze on the porch. "Lynn's father built it himself. He paid for it. Lynn grew up in it. But Rebecca inherited it. Maybe it was just the principle of the thing. But Lynn thought it should be half hers."

"So it's paid for?"

"Yes. For years."

"It can't be worth much."

"In money, no. In sentiment, yes."

"And what would your mother have done with this wonderful piece of nostalgia if it *was* half hers?"

Julie bit her lower lip before answering. "I don't know. Maybe she meant to charge Rebecca some sort of rent. I didn't ask, I found it all too upsetting."

He started the car, turned the corner to head back to Main Street. "I see," he said.

Julie laid her hot forehead against the cool glass of the window. How could he see when she herself could not? And what could the disagreement about the house have to do with Rebecca's disappearance?

Jake broke the silence. "You don't find it odd that your mother and Rebecca were never close?"

"Of course not," Julie muttered, closing her eyes. "There's a fourteen-year age difference between them. I'm fourteen years younger than my brother Sim, and sixteen years younger than Clark, Jr. We've never been close, either."

"Yeah," he said softly. "I keep forgetting you were the caboose in your family. You were quite a surprise to your parents, I'd guess."

"To say the least," she answered wryly. Just when her parents thought their parenting duties were almost over, Julie had come along, totally unexpected. And unlike the boys, Julie had not been obedient and conforming.

She kept her eyes closed, her forehead against the window. She was suddenly tired to the bone.

"Jules?" She remembered how he'd laughed when he'd first heard her brothers' boyish nickname for her. Then he adopted it. But she wished with all her heart he hadn't used it now. It made her think of times she'd tried for so long to forget. She squeezed her eyes more tightly shut.

"Jules?" he repeated, concern in his voice. "Are you all right?"

"I'm fine," she lied.

"We'll be at the motel soon," he said softly, "Then you can rest."

I can never rest when you're near me, she thought fatalistically.

But without him, how could she ever find Rebecca?

THERE WERE PLENTY of vacancies at the Black Gold Motel.

Jake saw that the motel, like Rebecca's house, had known better days. Its white stucco units needed painting and had turned a cracked, dirty gray. In the grassless verge in front of the office stood a tilted For Sale sign that had a forlorn air, as if it were doomed to stand there forever.

Jake checked in; they were assigned units thirteen and fourteen. There was only one other car besides theirs, parked before unit one.

He opened the trunk, and Julie hauled out her battered suitcase, not wanting his help.

"Give me that," he said firmly. "Do you want to rupture yourself?"

They had a short tug-of-war over the suitcase, which he, of course, won. He carried it to unit fourteen, unlocked the door and went in. He set the suitcase on the ancient, webbed contraption designed to hold it, which stood near the foot of the bed.

He tried to keep from looking at the bed itself or to imagine Julie in it, warm and naked between the sheets.

She stood in the doorway, looking drawn and uneasy. She carried her purse over her shoulder, clenching and unclenching her hands in a nervous gesture.

He made his way to the door and she pressed up against the doorframe to let him pass. When he stopped beside her, she looked up at him with something akin to alarm.

"Hey, Bambi-eyes," he said gruffly. "Don't look at me as if I'm the big, bad wolf. I told you I wouldn't touch you unless you wanted me to. I meant that. Here's your key."

He tossed it to her, and she caught it neatly. He didn't want his fingers brushing hers, even by chance.

"Lock your door. Use the dead bolt. I'm right next door—if you should want me."

He tore his gaze from her face and forced himself to leave her. He heard the door squeak as she closed it, shutting him out. The dead bolt slid into place with a muted click.

He pulled his suit bag from the trunk and threw it over his shoulder, then heaved the duffel bag out, walked to the door of unit thirteen and unlocked it.

The door swung open to reveal a room exactly like Julie's in every way—except the crack in the wall was in a different place. Hers was to the left of the window, from sill to ceiling. His was to the right, snaking from sill to floor.

There was blocky blond oak furniture that must have been new when Elvis was young and thin, a dimming mirror screwed to the wall and a double bed. The bedspread was a sickly color that might once have been blue, matching the equally sickly-looking drapes.

There was a faded print of an oil derrick against the sunset on the wall and a television set in the corner.

He threw his duffel bag on the bed and hung his suit bag in the cramped closet. What a waste, he thought. Two adults who made love like they'd invented it, locked into separate identical, solitary rooms.

What good was a double bed with only one person to sleep in it? And how wasted a shower was, if you could only use it to suds yourself down alone.

At least there *was* a shower, and he wanted one. He hadn't taken time to change his clothes, and he'd worn these two days in a row. He hated doing that, it made him uncomfortable.

Unbuttoning his shirt, he went to the bathroom and switched on the light. The bathroom was as lackluster as the rest of the place. The sink was chipped, the floor had squares of tile missing. The shower was designed for the Thin Man at the circus, and a large dead insect lay near the drain, its fragile legs in the air as if it had died praying to be taken to some better place.

He wrinkled his nose in distaste and unbuttoned his shirt the rest of the way. He was about to lean over and remove the dead insect from the Thin Man's shower, when he heard the shower turned on next door, in Julie's unit.

He groaned and leaned one hand on the sink, his other on his bare stomach, right above the fly of his jeans. He closed his eyes and imagined her under the sluicing water. Yearning shot through him like a hot spear.

He knew every delicious inch and curve of her body, and in his mind's eye, he could see it with painful clarity. Her body was neither too hard with muscle nor too soft from lack of it—its tone was feminine and perfect. To touch her when she was wet in the shower was like touching a petal in the rain.

Round white breasts tipped with pink, flawless and ex-quisite to touch. Her back was wide, which made her small waist seem all the smaller, and the rounded flair of her hips more exciting in contrast to her waist. He ached to run his hands over her body, to touch its most secret places, to give her and himself the most intense pleasure.

In the shower, her hair would seem even blacker, and it would flatten into long ribbons that clung to her naked shoulders, back and breasts.

After they showered together and made love, he some-times helped her brush her long hair dry, and more often than not, they would both get excited before it was over, and end up making love again.

The hushed rumbly sound of the water next door sud-denly ceased. He sighed with both relief and frustration. She was stepping out of the shower now, rosy and drip-ping, water beading her lashes into starry points. And now she was picking up the towel and . . .

He opened his eyes and stared at his reflection in the yellowed mirror. "You damned fool," he said with contempt.

What in hell was he doing to himself? If he wanted to torture himself, why didn't he just go out and lie on a hill of fire ants? He needed a shower, all right, an ice-cold one, at that.

He reached into the stall to turn on the cold water, full force. He wanted it to feel like a liquid glacier when he stepped into it.

He wrenched the faucet so hard that it came off in his hand with a grinding, shuddery whine. The water did not gush out. A feeble dribble started, then died to a weary, irregular drip.

He stared numbly at the faucet that now lay in his open hand. It was so corroded it had broken from the force of his angry twist. *Welcome to Casino,* he told himself.

He turned and looked at the sink again. It was small, tiny, in fact. He could wash his face, then daintily splash some water into his armpits, like one of those oil paintings of ladies who wash with a bowl and pitcher. That was about it—definitely not his style.

He strode into the room, picked up the telephone and dialed the office. He waited eight rings for an answer. "Yes?" said a bored-sounding voice. It was the withered, sour-looking little man that Jake remembered at the desk.

"This is Good Thunder in unit thirteen," Jake snarled. "The shower faucet just came off in my hand. How am I supposed to take a shower?"

For a moment, silence was his only answer. "Mister, I'm sorry. There's not a whole lot I can do. I'll reduce your bill. A five-buck refund, how's that?"

"I don't want five bucks," he snapped. "I want a shower. Put me in another unit."

"I can't, mister. They're all rented."

"How can they all be rented?" Jake demanded. "There was only one other car in the lot, dammit."

"Don't you go cursin'. You got no leave to curse. You can go down the road a hundred miles or so and stay someplace else if you got a mind to curse."

"I'm sorry," he said through gritted teeth. "But how can all the units be rented? Just give me another one, all right?"

The voice grew high with righteous complaint. "I *cain't* give you another. There is no more. I'm remodeling so's the place'll sell. I only got four units open—one and two is finished up, and thirteen and fourteen, which I ain't touched. The rest is all tore up. I'm workin' on 'em. *And* I just rented number two to a long-distance truck driver. That's why it took me so long to answer the phone."

"Then how do I take a shower?" Jake demanded, feeling the veins on his neck begin to stand out. "How about I come up to your place and take one, buddy?"

"I don't hold with showers. They is more stimulatin' than soothin', and they rustle up the blood. Mine broke and I never had it fixed. You want to come up and use the bathtub, that's fine. But hurry up. Everything is done rented, and I'm turnin' off the sign and goin' to bed."

Jake wanted to tell the old coot what to do with his bathtub, when suddenly an idea, beautiful, complex and complete as a fully opened rose, bloomed in his mind. *In the midst of every problem there is opportunity.* Hadn't Einstein said that?

He didn't have to be Einstein to see what the opportunity was. "No," he said, making his voice as conciliating as possible. "No, I won't trouble you. Sorry to have bothered you. You go right ahead. Shut off the lights and turn in. Sweet dreams."

He hung up the phone and listened to the silence. There was no sound from Julie's unit. There was no sound from anywhere, except the occasional dismal drip in the shower.

Julie was probably in one of those white nightgowns she used to wear—low-cut with little lacy straps. She was probably sitting on the edge of her bed, brushing and blow-drying her hair.

He counted to a hundred by ones to calm himself. Then he stuck the room key in the pocket of his jeans, gathered up some clean clothes, the towels, and the broken faucet.

He opened his door, let it ease shut and lock itself, then went to her door and raised his fist to knock. He paused, counted to a hundred by tens, then beat smartly on her door.

He held his breath until it inched open. Julie peered out suspiciously. He caught the fragrance of soap and shampoo, saw the gleam of her wet hair, and his heart leaped, his groin tightened.

"What?" she asked, looking him up and down.

He took a deep breath. Holding out the broken faucet for her to inspect, he said, "The shower's broken in my place. Can I use yours?"

She shook her head and look disgusted. "Oh, really, Jake, that's such a cheap trick. Just call the office. Have them put you into another unit."

"There is no other unit," he said, and he began to talk as fast as he'd ever talked to any drug dealer when trying to save his skin and not blow his cover.

He told her everything the wizened desk clerk had said, except, of course, that he had invited Jake to take a bath.

"If he hasn't got a shower, go use the bathtub," she said stubbornly. She looked adorable when she was stubborn.

"It's too late, he's turned in," Jake said.

As if decreed by fate, at that moment the neon sign that said Black Gold Motel winked off. The Vacancy sign magically changed to No Vacancy. And the lights in the office itself went out.

Julie stared out the door at the office in disbelief.

"How about it?" Jake asked, as innocent and earnest as he could be. "Be a Good Samaritan."

"You probably broke that faucet on purpose."

"I swear by all that's holy I didn't."

"Nothing's holy to you."

"Look at it," he said, holding it out to her again. "It took years to corrode like that. What do you think? I planned this for decades? It was an accident."

She gave him a dubious look.

"Come on," Jake pleaded. "Have mercy. We've been on the road all day. I never even took time to change my clothes. You know how I hate that. Let me use the shower. Then I'll leave. I swear it."

Unless you ask me to stay.

He held his breath again, and felt his heart beating so hard it shook his rib cage.

"All right," she said at last. "Just take the shower and get out. No funny business."

Unsmiling, she opened the door wide enough to let him in.

He nodded his gratitude and made no smart remark, gave her no knowing smile. He headed straight for the shower.

But even the coldest water couldn't wash away the image of her, standing there proud and reluctant, her damp black hair cascading down the skimpy bodice of the white nightdress.

Julie, Julie, Julie, he thought, his teeth clenched against the rush of the icy water. *Did any man ever want a woman as much as I want you?*

6

JULIE STOOD, brush in hand, and listened to the water run in the shower. The hard throb of her pulse seemed strange and irregular, following no steady beat.

She imagined Jake standing under the steady rush of the water, the streams pouring, crystalline, off his bronze skin. He was beautiful naked, muscular without being brawny, as well-proportioned as a classical statue.

She caught her breath painfully, remembering. When they used to shower together, which they did almost every night, she could not raise her eyes to his face without water blinding her, but she could gaze to her heart's content at the rest of him.

She'd liked touching his body, so hard, sun-darkened and different from her own. She could almost feel her fingers gliding across his powerful shoulders, trailing over the bulge of his biceps, down to the exquisite, strong bones of his wrists, then back again. She would press her lips against the warm, smooth flesh of his chest, kissing his heartbeat as the water cascaded over them.

Now he was only a few yards away from her, with only the bathroom door separating them. It would be so easy to slip out of her nightgown, to pad barefoot to the door and softly enter.

She could open the shower and slip inside, put her hands on his shoulders and press her mouth against his chest, just like she used to in the old days. He would welcome her, she knew. His wet, strong arms would wind around her, pulling her close. His mouth would close over hers, and the clean water would trickle, diamond-bright, over their faces.

Swiftly she turned away from the closed door, her cheeks burning. He had planned this, she knew. He meant to taunt her with memories.

"Hygiene and foreplay," he used to tease, stroking soap over her body. "Who could ask for anything more?"

Once she had flippantly replied, "Chocolate." The next night when they stepped out of the shower onto the fluffy bath mat, he took out a box of chocolate truffles from the medicine chest, where he had hidden it.

They took turns feeding each other the rich chocolates and drying each other's bodies. It was wicked. It was wonderful.

After that, it was a different sort of chocolate for every night of the week. She remembered sighing happily as one night he wrapped the big white towel around her. She'd leaned back against him as he gently massaged her shoulders, and breasts. As he'd brought a chocolate to her mouth, she'd whispered, "Raspberry creme. It must be Tuesday."

In bed he was an intense, inventive lover, and if he did not always tell her his feelings in words, he did so with a hundred loving actions. His mouth might never whisper sweet nothings, but it lavished sweetness on her body until she shivered with pleasure.

Oh, I can't remember that, I won't remember that, the censoring part of her mind said. What had existed between them hadn't been love. It hadn't lasted, it couldn't last. He and she had been too different, far too different. All they'd had was sex.

The more truthful part of her mind countered, *Yes. But what sex it was.*

She went to the tiny, cramped closet and took a long-sleeved cambric shirt from a hanger. She had no robe, so she put on the shirt and buttoned it right up to the chin. Then, for good measure, she buttoned the cuffs, too.

She turned and looked in the mirror. She had no makeup on, but her cheeks were vivid pink. Her hair, almost dry, hung loose to her waist. He'd always loved to toy with her hair. He said he was drawn to it as a moth to a flame. She went to the dresser and quickly began to pin it into a severe French twist.

The bathroom door opened, and she saw his reflection in the mirror. He paused in the doorway, looking at her. He wore different jeans, and a cotton shirt of a plaid so dark she couldn't tell if it was green or blue.

A fog of warm, steamy air, fragrant with the motel's Ivory soap, seeped from the bathroom. Jake's damp, dark hair hung over his forehead, and he hadn't buttoned up his shirt completely. She could see the spot on his chest that she had always kissed.

Shaken by the memory, she could almost taste that spot, feel its hardness against her lips. The sensation made her so nervous, she dropped a hairpin. It bounced on the glass surface of the dresser with a little *ping*, then lay still.

"Thanks," he said. "I feel like a new man."

She nodded, not trusting herself to speak. She picked up the hairpin and concentrated on pushing it into place.

"What are you doing?" His voice was low. Was there really an intimate, hungry growl in it, or was it only her imagination?

"I'm putting my hair back," she said as carelessly as she could. She reached for another pin, but dropped it, too. It hit the dresser top and bounced onto the shabby carpet.

She should have stooped to retrieve the pin, but she didn't. She would wait until he was gone. But he didn't leave. He stepped beside her, knelt and picked up the hairpin himself.

He looked up at her, his eyes as black as jet. "Why are you pinning your hair back before you go to sleep?" he asked. "You never do that."

"I do now," she lied.

He stayed where he was, one knee on the ground. It occurred to her that he looked like a knight there, kneeling before her. He offered her the hairpin as if it were a tribute.

"It'll come undone," he said. "You know how you toss around in your sleep. Why don't you put it in a braid if you want it out of the way? The way you used to?"

Damn you, she thought, gazing down at him. *What are you doing to me?*

He knew too much about her, even what she was like in her sleep. He said she dreamed more than anyone he'd ever heard of. She turned and twisted and murmured all night long.

In contrast, he slept as motionlessly as a man under an enchantment. She always fell asleep in his arms, but he couldn't keep hold of her. She'd twist or roll away. He said embracing her in her sleep was like trying to hug a giant jumping-bean.

His gaze fell to her shirt. "Why're you all buttoned up? Are you cold?"

"Yes," she said, which was half-true. She was by turns hot and cold all over, first feverish, then shivery.

"I've got a sweater in my room," he said. "Do you want me to bring it to you?"

"No," she said. *Stop being so sweet to me*, she wanted to cry.

She clenched the hairpin so hard she could feel her fingernails digging into her palm. She found it difficult to draw a breath, it stuck in her throat like a stone.

"Why are you staying on your knees like that?" she demanded, hating the curtness in her voice.

He raised his eyes to her face again. "It seems the right place for me to be. At your feet."

"Don't be ridiculous," she said, and turned her back on him. "Get your things and go."

She went to the door, ready to turn the knob and fling it open.

He rose with a sigh. He went back into the bathroom, returned with his used clothing draped over his arm. He paused by the door, his eyes meeting hers again.

"I left the towels. I reckon I'll need them again in the morning. Why drag them back and forth?"

"In the morning?" Julie said. "Isn't that a bit presumptuous? I haven't given you lifetime permission to use my shower."

"I always shower in the morning," he said. "You must remember."

"I don't remember at all," she said. She was conscious that her hair was starting to spill down from its incomplete pinning, and a long strand tickled her shoulder.

He smiled, and when he did, she felt as if he'd shot her through the heart. He reached out automatically to touch her hair, then stopped, as if his hand had frozen in midmotion.

Oh, God, she thought, looking at the fine shape of that hand, remembering its touch.

Images came to her in a flood—how they had made love for the first time, back in Oklahoma City, in what now seemed like a different life. They'd been out to dinner, then ended up at her place, supposedly to have coffee.

They both knew they'd soon be up in bed together. They knew it, and they took it sweet and slow.

She'd worn her hair swept up that night. At one point, as they sat on the couch, talking and nuzzling and forgetting about the coffee, a tendril had come loose, and she'd raised her hand to fasten it back in place.

His left hand closed over hers. "No," he'd said, kissing her lips, lightly, yet lingeringly. "Let me."

And one by one he'd drawn the pins from her hair, setting them carefully aside. With each strand of hair that fell softly free, he'd given her a slow, teasing kiss, on the ear, on the throat, on the lips, on the eyelids.

She'd been mad for him by the time he'd finished; she had never wanted a man so badly in her life. But he'd taken her face between his hands and said, "We've only started, Julie."

That memory shook her profoundly as she stared up at him now in this plain little motel room. She felt stricken with loss and want. He looked solemn and expectant, more handsome than ever.

"I said I wouldn't touch you unless you want me to," he breathed. "That was the agreement. Do you want me to?"

Desire swept her like fire, and something withered and died quietly in its force. Perhaps what died within her was her conscience or her pride. Or perhaps it was merely foolish inhibition.

"Yes," she whispered, her mouth trembling. "Take down my hair, Jake."

His fingers reached to her hair and slowly, expertly removed a pin. He opened her hand and placed it in her palm. Then he lowered his mouth to hers.

"We've only begun, Julie," he said and kissed her.

HE FELT like the runner in the last mile of a long, grueling race, weakness warring with willpower.

His weakness was her. It always had been, perhaps always would be. His will was to win her back by loving her as she had never been loved before. Wanting her was an urgent fire burning away his reason, but he constrained himself to take things slowly.

She'd said all that ever existed between them was sex. He meant to show her how sweetly shattering sex could be when it was wedded to love.

Her brown eyes seemed huge and frightened and luminous in the soft lamplight. Her beautiful mouth was slightly open, tremulous and glistening.

He willed his hand to be steady as he let down another strand of her hair. It uncoiled beneath his fingers like a wide ribbon of silk, falling to rest against her breast. He touched the side of her face lightly, letting his thumb trace the line of her lower lip with mothlike gentleness.

He lowered his mouth to hers and kissed her again, and she gasped with pleasure. He drew back and saw the desire in her eyes and thought, *Yes, Julie, this is what we can't escape. And no one will ever love you the way I do. No one.*

It took all his strength to continue at such a leisurely pace; it was driving him mad. But lock by lock he freed her lovely hair, and kiss by kiss he wooed her.

When, at last, her dark hair spilled like a river over her shoulders and down her back, he threaded his fingers through it, cradling the back of her head so he could bring his lips down upon hers with the utmost intimacy.

Her hand fluttered to his cheek and settled there. "Oh, Jake," she whispered in a shaking voice. "Oh, Jake."

Her touch, her breathlessness inflamed him, but he steeled himself not to hurry. His tongue slowly explored the moist silk of her inner mouth, flirting with her, teasing her, daring her to be bolder.

He raised his right hand to her collar and undid her top button. He drew his fingers across the delicate sculpture of the hollow of her throat, feeling the tripping rhythm of her pulse.

"Jake, I can't stand it," she said with a sensual sigh. And her fingers were unbuttoning his shirt, all the way, quickly and expertly. Her smooth, cool hands were on his chest, caressing him, and his heart began to buck in his chest like a stallion.

He undid her second button and trailed his fingers down the warm valley between her breasts. He kissed her more deeply. He felt as if he were falling through the darkness of outer space, drawn by her female gravity, lost to it, no longer in control of himself.

"Jake," she said in a pleading voice. "Please love me—now."

She undid the snap of his jeans, drew down his zipper, touched him.

He gasped, and his self-control went up in flames. But it was all right because hers had, too. Not bothering with her buttons, he pulled the shirt open, causing the buttons to rip loose like the tides of desire that drove him.

He pulled her lacy straps down, burying his face between her breasts. She fought her way out of the top of the nightgown, and he heard another soft, tearing sound as it fell around her waist.

"Don't touch me yet," he said between gritted teeth. "I can't stop if you touch me."

"I don't want you to stop," she almost whimpered and held him so close that he had to take a desperate, ragged breath, like a drowning man.

He carried her to the bed, ripping off his shirt. He kicked off his boots, struggled out of his jeans. She had already drawn off the torn nightgown and flung it aside.

Their bodies joined with an urgent inevitability, and he held her as tightly as he could, saying her name like a prayer as she welcomed him into her body. He thrust as deeply as he could, again and again.

He felt her body's answering ecstatic pulse, and he gave himself to her completely, while his blood thundered in his ears like the a war drum.

SHE HAD odd, disjointed dreams all night long. When she started to wake, drowsiness tried to charm her back to sleep. She half succumbed, snuggling through the twisted sheets to nestle securely against Jake's long, warm body.

Jake? Her eyes flew open in alarm. She sat up and stared down at him, aghast. In a rush, memories of last night came back, staining her cheeks with embarrassment.

Her gaze flew around the room. Her nightdress, one strap torn loose, lay beside the bed. Her cambric shirt, now buttonless, was flung carelessly on the dresser.

His jeans were a wrinkled heap at the foot of the bed. His shirt, torn, too, was lying in the bathroom doorway. She could see only one of his boots.

And here she was in a cheap motel, naked as a jaybird and apparently just as shameless. She jerked the sheet up to cover herself, a gesture of modesty that she realized was far too late.

She looked at Jake again, and suddenly she felt no shame. Instead, she felt an odd pleasure that was beyond right or wrong.

He slept as he always had, on his side, facing her, as motionless as a statue. The skewed sheet was draped over his pelvis and hips, but his torso and his long legs were naked. Against the white of the sheets, he looked like a sleeping warrior cast from bronze.

An artist to the core, she could not deny that he was good to look at, very good. His skin had a smooth, burnished sheen and was marred only at his thigh by the gunshot scar.

His beard was not heavy, but its shadow darkened the clean lines of his jaw. His hair, blue-black, darker even than hers, fell over his forehead almost boyishly. But his face was strong and clean with nothing childish about it.

Oh, Lord, she thought helplessly. *Here I am, on the edge of falling in love with him again. Wasn't once enough? Won't I ever learn?*

She pushed her hair out of her eyes and gazed at him sadly. With a sinking, sickening sensation of guilt, she wondered what she was going to do now.

She thought of Rebecca and her guilt increased a hundredfold. How could she have forgotten her aunt so completely?

She remembered her eagerness to be loved last night, and her cheeks flamed more hotly. She had wanted him with a passion as elemental as the need for air. No, she had wanted him more. She would have sold her soul to be with him last night.

Perhaps she had, she thought darkly. It was as if she'd used Rebecca's tragedy as an excuse to bring Jake back into her life, to satisfy the desire that no one else could satisfy.

Jake's dark lashes fluttered, his eyes opened and he turned his face up to hers, meeting her gaze. He reached out to stroke her cheek, but she dodged his caress.

"Don't," she said and clutched the sheet closer to her breasts.

"Uh-oh," he said, letting his arm drop back to the sheets. "I know that look. Guilt already? What's wrong, Jules?"

Don't call me Jules, she thought, angry at him as well as herself. *Don't act like everything's just the way it used to be—it's not.*

He stretched lazily, like a big cat. But when he sat up straight, bracing himself on one arm, his expression was serious. "You can't really regret last night," he said.

"I do," she said, looking away.

"Hey," he said softly. "We made the earth move. Also Mars, Mercury, Venus, Neptune, Uranus, Jupiter and Pluto. Did I leave any out?"

"Saturn," she said unhappily.

"We definitely moved Saturn," he said. "Probably spun its rings off. If not the first time, the second."

"Ohhh," she moaned and put her hand to her forehead. It hadn't been bad enough to make love with such abandon only once. Oh, no, they'd done it twice, going at it like minks.

"Julie," he said, "I told you I wouldn't touch you unless you wanted me to. You said you did. You can't deny it was good. More than good. Look at me."

She let her gaze, regretful, meet his somber one.

He sighed again. "This is about Rebecca, isn't it? You're feeling guilty because of your aunt."

"Partly," she said. "But it's more than that. There's you and me. It can never work, you see, because—"

He placed his forefinger against her lips, silencing her. "That's a conversation for later," he said.

"But it doesn't seem right—"

"Shh," he said, his voice gentle. "Listen to me. Maybe what we have *can't* last. It's still a gift, isn't it?"

She shrugged. She was unsure if the physical passion between them was gift or curse.

"We're consenting adults. There is nothing wrong with this. Nothing unnatural. Nothing shameful."

"Right," she said bitterly. "It's simply chemistry, that's all."

"Don't talk like that," he said, an edge in his voice. "Give me your hand."

She shook her head. "It'll do no good—"

"My God, Julie," he said, "last night you gave me everything—this morning you won't even give your hand? What kind of hypocrisy is that?"

He was right, she knew. It was not that she didn't care for him. But caring for him was so dangerous. She gave him a wan smile and slipped her hand into his. Her heart took a forbidden skip.

He smoothed her hair. "You think we were disrespectful to Rebecca? Yesterday you were sad because Rebecca never had what you and I share. Isn't that a little contradictory?"

Her smile died as she stared at their joined hands. "And isn't that a little too slick, Jake? You always could argue that black was white and make people believe it. It's your business to make people believe things."

He squeezed her fingers and for a moment, he didn't answer. Then he said, "Lying's not my business. Justice is. Sometimes I lie to get justice done. It's a paradox, but that's how it is."

"How it is," Julie murmured, "is too complicated. I feel I've wronged Rebecca. You can't argue about feelings."

He bent nearer and looked into her eyes. "How it is, Julie, is that it happened. Life goes on. If I've learned one thing being a cop, it's that. Life goes on. It's supposed to."

She shook her head. "I can't accept that."

He took her chin between his fingers and thumb. "You have to. Wherever Rebecca is, mourning won't bring her back. Neither will chastity or anything else except what you're doing now—looking for her."

Julie looked away again. "I hardly call trying to hit ten on the sexual Richter scale 'looking for her.'"

He turned her face back to his. "Jules, that's exactly what I mean. You can't look twenty-four hours a day. If it's possible to find Rebecca, I'll find her for you. I swear that."

She felt the tears rising in her eyes and willed them not to spill. "You can't promise such a thing. You don't know."

"I promise it for you," he said earnestly. "I'll find her. Do you believe me?"

She stared at him, the implacable passion in his eyes, the determined, almost severe set of his mouth.

"I believe you," she whispered in spite of herself.

"Then prove it," he breathed. "Kiss me good morning."

She hesitated, but found herself raising her lips to his. *Oh, Rebecca*, she thought. *Please forgive me.*

7

JAKE HAD NOT TEMPTED Julie beyond that single kiss.

He knew she was poised on some delicately balanced perch within herself. One wrong move, and the balance could break and fall against him. He would be careful and not push her. He would go slowly.

But he wanted the good-morning kiss because it linked this morning to last night; he would not let last night be isolated, he didn't want her locking it away from the present. He wouldn't let her.

Otherwise, he tried to seem casual, let events flow in an ordinary course. They took turns in the shower; he went first so he could go back to his room, getting out of her space for a little while. He acted solemn, but in his heart he was blessing the Saint of Faulty Faucets and giving thanks to Rebecca.

Rebecca, he thought as the water sluiced over him in a crystal rush, *I owe you. I said I'll do right by you, and I will.*

Later that morning, in the office of Sheriff Donnie Luffmiller, Jake realized the extent of his promise.

"It's a mystery, sure as shootin'," said Donnie Luffmiller, never taking his eyes from Julie. He'd obviously been smitten from the moment she'd walked in the door.

Julie looked crestfallen. Jake knew she was further troubled because the sheriff hardly inspired confidence. Luffmiller was a slim, red-haired man with a cowlick, freckles, jug ears, and he looked no more than eighteen.

Luffmiller smiled boyishly at Julie, but his small blue eyes looked sly. "I got a new lead, and I won't pull no stops trying to run it down. We're lookin' for that fiancé of hers. He may be the key to all this."

Jake's nerve endings prickled. He glanced at Julie, who sat, arms crossed, staring at Luffmiller in disbelief.

"Fiancé?" Julie's face was the picture of shock. "What fiancé? My aunt was never engaged."

"She was engaged, ma'am," Luffmiller said, looking like a smug schoolboy. "Two years ago. And that's a fact."

Jake thought, *Wait a minute. This does not compute.*

"Hold on," Jake said, frowning. "This fiancé—who is he? Why haven't we heard of him before?"

The sheriff's youthful face was cool and superior. "Well, now, he is the new lead I'm checkin' out. What I'm giving you is privileged information. Out of deference to Miz FitsJames here." He nodded toward Julie and gave her a winning smile.

Jake was swept by the depressing realization that he was dealing with a complete jackass. The fool was trying to impress Julie, and in a way he had done it. She was obviously stunned.

Jake's options fanned out in his mind like a hand of cards. He *wanted* to explode, probably making Luffmiller wet his pants. Normally, Jake would limit himself to emitting dangerous vibes and demanding the whole truth—fast. But instinct told him that Luffmiller could be played best by flattery.

"By the look on Miss FitsJames's face, you have plumb taken her breath away," Jake said. "This puts a whole new color on things. Who is this fiancé? How come nobody knew about him before?"

The sheriff sat, his eyes glued on Julie, his chest puffed up like a pigeon's. "This is late-breaking news. We just found out about him. From Miz Charity Klopp. You aunt played it close to the chest, Miz FitsJames."

"How late did this news break?" Jake asked. He didn't bother to keep the sarcasm out of his voice. Luffmiller was obviously too in love with himself to notice.

"Yestiddy," Luffmiller said, never taking his eyes from Julie. "Miz Klopp called us yestiddy. She just came back to town. To see her grandma."

"You've told the state police and Austin?" Jake said.

"'Course I have. Soon as I heard. This is confidential, by the way, Miz FitsJames. You understand that?"

Julie, still looking dumbstruck, nodded. Smooth as silk, Jake said, "Certainly she understands. Words can hardly express her gratitude. Can you tell her more?"

Luffmiller squared his shoulders importantly. "This fiancé's name is George O'Keefe. Your aunt met him during summer vacation, two years ago. It was a sorta whirlwind courtship."

Julie blinked. "Rebecca? In a whirlwind courtship? She never said a word about it to me."

Luffmiller unsuccessfully tried to seem sympathetic, but only ended up looking like a gangly adolescent full of lust and conceit. "I don't imagine she did tell you, ma'am. She didn't admit it to nobody. Except Miz Klopp. Sounds like he was nothin' but a flimflam man, and he took her to the cleaners. To the tune of twenty-five thousand dollars. Took the money and run, he did."

"Twenty-five thousand dollars?" Julie echoed. "Some—some con man took her for twenty-five thousand dollars?"

"Ten thousand dollars of it in cash," Luffmiller said. "We checked with the bank. She made the withdrawal, all right. I'm sorry to be the bearer of bad news."

But Luffmiller didn't look sorry. He looked as if he was suppressing a grin as wide as the Cheshire cat's.

Julie's eyes flashed. "She gave ten thousand dollars to this—this George O'Keefe? And then she turned around and gave fifteen thousand dollars to this other outfit—Norcross and Associates? I don't believe it. My aunt was not a stupid woman."

"I'm sure she wasn't," Luffmiller said with a smirk. "But she was a lady at—how can I put it?—at a certain stage of life. I reckon she wasn't hittin' on all cylinders."

"Menopause?" Julie retorted. "It's not a mental disease. When a woman turns fifty, she doesn't automatically go insane. Rebecca certainly didn't."

Luffmiller blushed to the roots of his orange hair, and Jake curbed a smile.

Luffmiller said, "I didn't mean anything personal, ma'am. Don't mistake me."

"Besides," Julie argued, "Rebecca didn't even *like* Charity Klopp. Why would she tell her such a personal thing?"

"They were friends from childhood," Luffmiller said in a high voice.

"They were *acquaintances* from childhood," Julie snapped.

"I'm just sayin' what she told me," Luffmiller protested. "Now listen. I figure this O'Keefe, he came back and ran a second scam on her. He talked her into investin' in this Norcross and Associates, which was nothing but a bunko scheme—"

"I can*not* believe this," Julie said. "I will *not believe* this."

Julie's spirit made Jake fall a little more in love with her, if that was possible. He said, "You've got the state police running a check on O'Keefe?"

"Of course," Luffmiller said, not to him, but to Julie. "They'll report as soon as they find anything. You want to know what's happening, you stay in touch with *me*."

Jake said, "This woman—Charity Klopp. You say she just got back in town? She's here now?"

"She's stayin' at her grandma's house," Luffmiller said. "It's the big house on First Street. I'll give you the address."

"I know where it is," Julie said.

"Where's Ms. Klopp been?" Jake asked. "Why did she just come forward with this information?"

"Miz Klopp lives in Santa Fe, New Mexico," Luffmiller said. "She didn't know nothing about your aunt's disappearance. She don't communicate a lot with anybody in town but her kin. Her grandma can't talk or write. She's done had a stroke."

"I think Miss FitzJames needs to talk to Ms. Klopp herself," Jake said. "You've been a great help, Sheriff. Thanks. Miss FitzJames will stay in touch with you." He discreetly elbowed Julie. "Won't you, Miss FitzJames?"

Julie had apparently been too concerned about Rebecca before to realize the sheriff had the hots for her, but she caught on now. She gave Luffmiller her most irresistible smile. Jake had trouble resisting it himself.

"I'll most certainly call you," she told Luffmiller. "You've been more help than everybody else put together. I can't thank you enough."

Luffmiller beamed. "You can depend on me, ma'am. Feel free to phone or drop by anytime."

"You're too good to me," Julie said.

"It's no trouble," Luffmiller said. "It's a pleasure."

Once outside the sheriff's office, Jake took Julie by the arm. "It took you a while to figure it out," he breathed in her ear. "Honey catches more flies than vinegar. Sheriff

Luffmiller fell in love with you at first sight. Treat him right, and whatever he knows is yours."

She didn't smile, and her eyes were troubled. "Jake, this is getting stranger all the time. Rebecca engaged? It makes no sense, none at all."

"I think," he said, "we need to talk to Charity Klopp."

JULIE REMEMBERED the big house on First Street. It was the mansion of the Higgins family, the descendants of J. D. "Flash" Higgins, the wildcatter who'd sunk the first oil well in Casino and who'd hit a gusher big enough to make himself and his family rich.

She watched Jake knock on the big oak front door. "What I said is true. Rebecca never liked Charity Klopp. Rebecca was a mild person—she was on good terms with everyone. Everyone, that is, but Charity Klopp. Why would she tell Charity her personal business?"

"We'll see," said Jake.

A Hispanic woman in a maid's uniform opened the door. "Yes?" she said.

Jake spoke to her fluently in Spanish, and the woman replied so quickly that Julie could not keep up. Jake said something about being the person who had called ahead, and that Señora Klopp was expecting them. The rest was lost on Julie.

The maid, at first stone-faced, ended up beaming at Jake as she let them into the house. She gave long, chattering answers to his questions, as if she had been waiting for years to speak in her own language again.

"What did you say to her?" Julie whispered when the woman left them standing in the foyer.

"I'll tell you later," he said.

Julie gazed up at him in puzzlement, but he was looking around the foyer as if he was memorizing it. The entry room was walled with marble, and a chandelier gleamed from above, even though morning burned brightly outside.

Julie thought that the house, although richly constructed, had something sad and abandoned about it. The carpet beneath her feet had once been luxurious, but now looked worn and quaint, like something that belonged in a museum. Dust motes floated through the still air, and Julie had a peculiar certainty that the house had possessed this useless, dead atmosphere even when Rebecca was young.

Then a door was flung open, and Julie had no more time to brood. A rail-thin woman with bleached blond hair stood in the central doorway, a cigarette in her hand.

"Darlings!" she said in a dramatic voice. "I'm Charity Higgins Klopp. You're here about dear Rebecca?"

Charity Klopp wore an expensive-looking pantsuit of cream-colored silk, and every part of her that could be covered with jewels, was. She was the only person Julie had ever seen who wore rings on her thumbs.

Her wrists were weighed down with bracelets, her neck stooped with them. Her earlobes sagged with pearls and garnets. She looked like a wrinkled child who had been playing dressup in a dime store.

"Come into my parlor, said the spider to the fly," Charity Klopp said with a nervous giggle. She still stood in the central doorway and nodded inward.

"Ms. Klopp," Jake said, all sleekness and charm. "It's a pleasure. I'm Jake Good Thunder, Oklahoma State Police. This is Julie FitzJames, Rebecca Albert's niece."

"Julie, Julie, Julie," Charity said melodramatically. "Rebecca always spoke of you. You were her pride, her joy. Come into the sitting room."

Numbly, Julie let Jake guide her into Charity's sitting room, which was large, shadowy and smelled of mildew. The walls were filled with shelves of books that looked unread, and the stiffly upholstered, old-fashioned chairs and sofas looked as if they hadn't been sat in for years.

"Sit, sit, sit," commanded Charity, waving her cigarette. "Oh, God, I know the room's a fright. The whole house is a fright. *I'm* a fright. What is one to do? 'Backward, oh, backward, turn time in thy flight.'"

With a strange, careless flop, she dropped into the room's central chair, which was as large as a throne and covered with dull gray velvet that looked mummified.

Jake nodded for Julie to sit on the matching velvet sofa. Sitting beside her, he focused all of his attention on Charity Klopp, who seemed to love it.

"Excuse my jewelry," she said, spreading her fingers so that all her rings flashed. "I reckon life is short, I should enjoy it as much as I can, while I can—*n'est-ce pas?*"

"*Mais oui,*" said Jake, slipping into French as smoothly as he had into Spanish. "*Ou la belle rêve est perdue. Mais, c'est encore vivante. Avec vous, madame.*"

Julie thought, my Lord but he was slick. What had he said? That a beautiful dream was still alive with the older woman? Had he no shame?

"*Excusez-moi,*" Charity said and took a fast suck on her cigarette. "I fall into French out of habit. Woodrow—my second husband—and I were in Belgium for six years with the oil business. Boy, it's hard to stay down on the farm, once you've seen Par-ee."

"*Je n'ai pas de doute,*" said Jake, and Julie resisted the urge to kick him to see if he was really human. "But you come back to Casino every year to see your grandmother? Very admirable."

Charity shrugged. "It's home. What can I say? But, God, it's a dismal town. Nobody stays. Except people like my grandmother, who've never known anything else. What we'll do with this dump when she dies, I've got no idea." She rolled her eyes.

"What about Rebecca Albert?" asked Jake. "Was she like your grandmother? Would she have stayed in this town, no matter what? Or do you think she may have simply taken off for someplace else?"

Charity ground out her cigarette in a marble ashtray and gave a nervous giggle. "Rebecca? She was as predictable as that thing in Yellowstone Park. What do they call it— Old Faithful? Trust me. I've known her since kindergarten."

She fumbled in the folds of her clothing and withdrew a pack of Winstons and a gold lighter.

"So," said Jake. "You don't think she just went off on her own."

"Absolutely not," Charity said as she lit a fresh cigarette. Her hand shook slightly. "She was the sort of person who was *not capable* of the unexpected. No, something's happened to her. It's horrible, but there's no doubt in my mind. Something's *happened*."

Julie's heart sank. She got the eerie feeling that Rebecca used to describe by saying, "A goose walked over my grave.'"

"Ms. Klopp," Jake said, "Sheriff Luffmiller said Rebecca told you she'd been engaged to a man and had given him ten thousand dollars. Can you tell us about that conversation?"

Charity exhaled and studied Jake through the blue cloud of her own smoke. "I come back to see Grandma once, twice a year. I'd move her to Santa Fe to have her nearer, but this is her home, it's where she's comfortable."

"Yes, ma'am," said Jake.

Charity tossed her head so that her pearl and garnet earrings flashed. "When I come back, I always try to see some of the gang from the old days. It's getting harder and harder. Everybody's moved away."

She picked a crumb of tobacco from her lip. "The last two years or so, only Rebecca was left of the old crowd. I asked her to lunch. I always like a nice bottle of wine with lunch, but Rebecca wasn't used to it. It went right to her head, and she started crying, right when Consuela set the custard dessert down in front of her. 'Charity,' she said, 'I'm afraid I've been a fool.' And then she told me."

"About this George O'Keefe?"

Charity nodded briskly. "Well, anyone but Rebecca would have seen right through him. But she was so inexperienced. So naive. A sitting duck. And her father hadn't been dead all that long. I suppose she was lonesome."

"How did she meet O'Keefe?" Jake asked. "And where? Did she tell you?"

"She'd gone into Austin for a poetry conference," Charity said, shaking her head. "You know Rebecca, always scribbling poetry. Well, she lost her wallet in the hotel gift shop, and *he* found it and returned it. One thing led to another."

"But that's totally unlike Rebecca," Julie said. "To pick up with a strange man."

Charity gave her a rather cold look. "My dear, when you reach a certain age, you look in the mirror and say, 'What have I done with my life?' I've asked myself that—and I've had three husbands. Think of Rebecca. Except for other people's children, her life was empty."

Julie thought of Rebecca and bit her lip, saying nothing.

Charity exhaled again and squinted at Jake through the smoke. "If you ask me, the whole thing was a setup. He was probably scouting that poetry conference, hoping to find some silly, romantic woman like Rebecca. I don't believe she ever lost her wallet. He probably picked it out of her purse himself, if you ask me."

"Ms. Klopp," Jake said, "this liaison between Rebecca and O'Keefe, it started in the summer?"

"It started in summer, it ended in summer," Charity said and adjusted a dry blond curl. "He got what he wanted and he disappeared. He *said* he was an account executive for a textbook company, that he was on the road a lot. He told her his money was all tied up in stocks and bonds. He wanted the twenty-five thousand from her to buy her a ring. Like a fool, she gave it to him. And then he was gone. Bye-bye, love."

Julie was shocked to see that Charity's face wore an expression of grim satisfaction, almost as if she relished Rebecca's bad luck. The woman mashed out her cigarette and reached for another. Taking her lighter from her, Jake lit the cigarette for her. She gave him an almost predatory smile.

Jake said, "She never filed a complaint against O'Keefe?"

"God, no," Charity said. "She was too humiliated. She said she never told anybody except me. And she begged me not to tell. And I didn't. Until she disappeared. Then I thought it was my duty."

"I see. When did she tell you?"

"Last August. The last time I was here to see my grandmother."

"You and Rebecca, you were always close?"

Charity gave a hoarse little laugh. "We've known each other since dinosaurs roamed the earth, for God's sake. We went to elementary school together. Kindergarten through eighth grade. We were in the same *Brownie* troop, believe it or not. As I said, the other girls have all drifted off. To the four corners of the earth. Liz Kelly's in Mexico. Annie Prewitt went clear to New Zealand. But she's dead, and now Rebecca's gone, too. My God, it seems like just yesterday we were all together. We were so young and innocent. How did all this happen? I need a drink. Do you want one?"

Julie shook her head and whispered, "No, thank you."

"No, thanks," Jake said. "You said Rebecca was humiliated. What do you think would have happened if O'Keefe turned up a second time in her life?"

Charity rose and went to a carved mahogany liquor cabinet. She took out a bottle of bourbon and poured herself a glass. She turned and looked at Jake.

"That's what I wonder. Because, embarrassed as she was, she said, 'I forgive him.' Those were her exact words. 'I forgive him. And I'd do it all over again.'"

Julie's blood chilled. *Had* Rebecca done it all over again? Had O'Keefe returned and talked her into investing in Norcross and Associates? Was he the man with the turquoise rings? Did he engineer her disappearance?

Charity tossed down her drink. "Women do foolish things for love," she said bitterly. "Take it from me."

Involuntarily, Julie's gaze turned to Jake, his dark hair and handsome profile. *Yes,* she thought, remembering her joyous abandon at being in his arms again, *it's true. Women do very foolish things for love.*

"WHAT A BARRACUDA," Jake said, opening the passenger door for Julie.

"She's nothing like Rebecca, nothing," Julie said. "It's hard to imagine them being children together."

Jake got in and put the key in the ignition. "It's hard to imagine Charity Klopp being a child at all. Let's go take a look at Rebecca's house."

Julie leaned her elbow against the door and pressed her hand against her forehead. She was deeply upset about George O'Keefe.

"Jake, I'm worried sick about this. Did she let that man use her, then come back and do it again? Was she that lonely? That desperate?"

"I don't know, sugar. That's what we're going to find out."

"She never said a word about him to me," Julie said, her voice choked. "She must have been too ashamed. Poor Rebecca—with nobody to turn to except Charity."

Jake frowned. "Charity said she went to elementary school with Rebecca. Not high school? Why?"

Julie sighed. "Oh, her parents sent her to private school in Austin. And then to college in the East."

"So she and Rebecca go back a long way. But they were hardly best friends."

"No. Rebecca's best friend was Annie Prewitt."

"The one in New Zealand who died?"

"Yes. Charity's right about that—they did spread out all over, those women. Everybody left Casino. Except Rebecca."

"After we look at Rebecca's house, I want to talk to the principal of her school. Do you know his name?"

"*Her* name," Julie said, her hand still pressed to her forehead. "Tammy Cummings. But she doesn't know Rebecca well. She just came to Casino. The other principal retired."

"That's a switch," he said. "Somebody coming to Casino."

"The sheriff's new, too," she said. "I remember the old one. He was quite the character. He wore an eye patch and looked like John Wayne in *True Grit*. This one looks eight years old."

"He's thirty," Jake said, stealing a searching glance at her. She sounded weary and disillusioned.

She rubbed her eyes. "Thirty? How do you know?"

"I read the date on his high school class ring, then did some math."

Her hand fell back to her lap and she gave him a small smile that made his heart leap. "You're good, Jake. You really are."

"It's my job," he said. "What happened to the old sheriff? And the former principal? I'd like to talk to them."

Julie's smile faded and she gave a hopeless shrug. "They did what everybody else does, I think. They moved away." She paused. "Jake, do you think the police will find George O'Keefe?"

"They'll do their best," he said. He himself felt uneasy about O'Keefe. The guy had most likely been using an alias, and if he made his living bilking women, he probably had a string of aliases and stayed on the move.

Yet something about Charity Klopp's story didn't sit right with him. "It's funny," he said, narrowing his eyes, "that Charity would remember the guy's name from clear back two years ago. My bet would be that the woman keeps her brain fogged up with alcohol as much as possible. Why would his name stick in her mind like that?"

Julie slipped her hand behind her neck and began to massage it. "George O'Keefe?" she said moodily. "It'd be hard to forget. It's so much like the artist, Georgia O'Keeffe. The woman who painted the flowers."

"That's natural for you to remember. But why would Charity Klopp?"

"Because her third husband runs an art gallery in Santa Fe," Julie said.

He turned the corner that led to Rebecca's street. Julie stared out the window at the houses, her face sad. Jake pulled into Rebecca's driveway, switched off the ignition and looked at Julie with concern.

He touched her cheek. "Hey. Are you up to this? Or is it going to be too hard on you?"

She turned to him, her brown eyes shimmering with unshed tears. "I want to find her, Jake. Nothing's going to be too hard if I can do that."

"Good girl," he said. He bent and kissed her, briefly and gently. She did not resist, but when he drew away, her face wore its haunted, guilty expression again.

JULIE STEELED herself as she unlocked the familiar door and swung it open. The house was dark, its front windows shaded by the porch. She flicked on the inside lights.

"The lights work," Jake said. "Who's paying the electric bill?"

"I am," Julie said. "I couldn't bear it if she came home and found her house all dark and sealed up like a t-tomb."

Her tongue stumbled on the word *tomb*, and she knew why. The more time that passed, the more she feared that something terrible had happened to Rebecca. The story about O'Keefe frightened her and made her see Rebecca's lonely life in a new and disturbing light.

"This is the living room," she said, making a helpless gesture. "You can see her plants. I—I couldn't bear to throw them out."

He nodded. Flowerpots lined the front windowsills, and crowded a pair of little tables placed near the windows. The African violets—Rebecca's pampered favorites—had turned to blackened, shriveled patches. Only a lone philodendron, its leaves turning yellow, had survived the neglect.

The house smelled stuffy and had an air of empty loss about it. Julie walked to the old upright piano. Its top was covered with a long crocheted rectangle, on which sat clusters of photographs in cheap frames.

She picked up an enlarged black-and-white snapshot, studied it meditatively, then offered it to Jake. "Look," she said. "Rebecca's Brownie troop. There's Charity in the back row. They must have been about seven when this was taken."

Jake studied the photo. "My God, it *is* Charity. She really was a child. Which one's Rebecca? This one?"

She shook her head. "No. That's Annie Prewitt. This is Rebecca, with the pigtails."

"They all look alike in those uniforms. Can you name them?"

"Not all of them," Julie said. She traced her finger along the back row. "There's Rebecca, Annie, Charity, and Liz Kelly. Liz married some executive in the oil business and, like Charity told us, lives in Mexico."

She moved her finger to the front row. "Let's see, that's Emily Wickett—no, that one's Emily Wickett, I forget where she lives now. I don't know who this girl is. It might be one of the Everinghams. I think it's Judy Sue. Everingham was the sheriff. He had a whole passel of daughters. I don't know this one, either."

Jake set the photo back into place, picked up another. "My Lord," he said, the corner of his mouth twitching into a smile. "It's you. Look at you."

Julie saw herself at eight years old, dressed up as a fairy princess for a school play and beaming shamelessly, extraordinarily proud of herself.

"Oh, yuck," she said. "Don't look at that. What a little priss I was. Here, this is my mother and me and Rebecca. Daddy took this, I remember."

Jake's smile faded. "Your mother *was* a looker. She did look like a movie star."

"Rita Hayworth, that's what everybody said," Julie said. Her mother stood, her hands on Julie's shoulders. She smiled brightly into the camera, but there was something contrived, professional about her smile. Julie's expression was shyly happy.

Rebecca, standing next to them, did not look at the camera but stared in obvious admiration at her beautiful older sister. Lynn's hair was long, falling past her shoulders in shining waves, her makeup was perfect, her figure tall and trim.

But Rebecca wore no makeup except lipstick, her hair was primly pulled back and she did not seem fourteen years younger than Lynn; plain and plump, she looked the same age or even older.

Jake shook his head. "Rebecca must have felt completely eclipsed. It couldn't have been easy, growing up in your mother's shadow."

"She never complained," Julie said. "But she wasn't the sort for complaining. She adored Lynn."

"Your mother always had a ton of boyfriends, I suppose."

"She certainly had her share."

"And Rebecca?"

Julie looked at her aunt's stocky figure and unremarkable face. "No one," she said sadly. "Rebecca never had a single suitor. At least, not that I know of."

Except George O'Keefe, she thought bitterly. *Oh, Rebecca, wouldn't no love at all have been better than that?*

"This is Rebecca again," he said, picking up another picture. "What is she, a bridesmaid? Who's getting married?"

Julie frowned slightly, trying to remember. "I think it was Annie Prewitt's wedding. She married, let me see, Thorgood Quaid. He was her first husband. He died in a car accident, I think. Then she married that man from New Zealand. Smith, I think his name was."

"She's a tiny thing," he said. "She's even thinner than Charity."

"Her nickname was Slim," Julie said. "And she called Rebecca 'Shmoo'—it was the only nickname Rebecca ever had. I have no idea what it means."

"I think a 'shmoo' was a cartoon character, sort of round and humble and good-natured and all-giving."

"Well, that would fit Rebecca," Julie said softly.

"She had a lot of pictures of you."

"My mother gave her my school picture for Christmas every year. That and a plant and things like bath powder. Not very original gifts, I'm afraid."

"The piano," he said, nodding at its yellowing keys. "She played it?"

"A little. Just enough to get by. My mother was the musician. She won a lot of prizes in her day."

Jake lifted one dark eyebrow. "And what did Rebecca win?"

"The attendance medal at Sunday school," Julie almost whispered. "She always tried to have perfect attendance."

Julie turned away from the pictures, unable to look any longer. "I think we should search her desk," she said, her chin quivering. "I tried to go through her papers before, but I was too—too—I couldn't think very well, I was too—"

She could not finish the sentence. She was afraid she was going to cry again. She put her hands to her face and took a deep, quivering breath.

"Oh, Jake, it's so awful. What if she's died without ever having had a chance to live? One love affair her whole life long—and it wasn't even real. But it was all she had."

She had sworn she wouldn't let him touch her in Rebecca's house. It had seemed sacrilegious to her.

But when Jake took her into his arms and held her tightly, it seemed right.

He said nothing, only held her. And she held on to him, too, pressing her face against his chest.

Don't make the some mistakes Rebecca did, the silence seemed to say.

What mistakes were those? she wondered, her head aching in confusion. Not loving enough? Or loving too desperately?

8

DAMMIT, REBECCA, ONE CLUE, Jake thought, frowning over the woman's papers. *Just give me one hint of what happened to you—for Julie's sake.*

He was worried about Julie; he'd never seen her this dispirited. It made him feel more than a little sick, to see her pain and not be able to ease it.

She was in the bedroom, going through Rebecca's closet. He sat at Rebecca's desk in the dining room, examining her records. She had been an orderly woman. Nothing was out of place.

He found her bills from years past, bundled up neatly and fastened together with rubber bands. Every month, like clockwork, she'd paid her bills.

With Julie's permission, he'd opened Rebecca's envelope of canceled checks from the bank. The last check she'd written had been on February fifteenth in Austin, at Munson's Shoe Outlet. They'd found the shoes, sensible brown ones, in her room, still in the box.

He went through the other canceled checks. She'd paid the gas, electric, phone, cable television and Visa bills. She'd left a balance of $388.87 in her checking account.

In the right-hand bottom drawer, he found personal letters she had saved. A stack from Julie. A postcard of the Eiffel Tower from Charity Klopp, postmarked two years ago. Five announcements that she'd received minor prizes in state poetry contests. The announcements were dated and spread over a two-year period.

And in the back, where he'd almost missed it, stuck sideways, a flowery greeting card with no envelope. He read the lines on the outside:

Thinking of you when the sun shines
Or when the raindrop is on the rose...

He opened the card.

Thinking of you always—
As my affection grows and grows!

It was signed in bold black pen, "All my love, George."

Jake's pulse sped up. Charity had been right. He set the card carefully aside, knowing it was probably impossible to lift prints from it.

Had Rebecca saved the card because it brought back memories? Or had she meant to throw it out, and it had escaped because it had been pushed to the back of the drawer?

He opened the bottom left-hand drawer. It was full of old checking records. He went through them mechanically. He found the entries for the three mysterious checks to Norcross and Associates. He saw the withdrawal of ten thousand dollars in July, two years ago.

If George took you, Rebecca, he thought, *did he take you for ten thousand? Or twenty-five? Did he come back again, one last time, trying to get the rest from you?*

There was plenty more George could have got: almost six thousand left in Rebecca's savings account, as well as the house itself, the source of so much dissension between Rebecca and her sister. If George was a con man worth his salt, why hadn't he wrung every dime from her he could?

And why had he taken two years to get what he got? It made no sense.

Unless, he thought, Rebecca had more than one lover. This idea went against everything Julie had ever said about the woman, but what if her affair with George had only whet her appetite? What if it had been the start of a sick addiction to being used?

Had she found another interested beau, who got her to invest in Norcross and Associates? Had she been picking up a third in the restaurant of the hotel, only this time she got more than she'd bargained for?

He found Rebecca's address book and went through the entries. There was no O'Keefe among them and no George. He saw the now-familiar names of her girlfriends. Liz Kelly Anderson; Judy Sue Everingham Fallon; Charity Higgins Klopp; Anna Prewitt Smith. Through Annie Prewitt's name and address was struck a shaky line. A notation beside it said, "My dear friend is gone. 'We will meet again at Heaven's Door.'"

Jake shut the book, put it back in the drawer. He rose and walked down the hall. Julie, pale and looking stricken, sat on Rebecca's bed. Objects from the closet lay heaped around her: purses, old photo albums, piles of magazines.

When she looked up at Jake questioningly, he said, "I found a mushy card signed 'All my love, George.' No date, no last name, no envelope, no return address. How about you?"

She picked up a magazine with a pastel green cover. "I'm reading Rebecca's poems in *Inheritance, A Journal of Texas Verse*. She was a fairly regular contributor." She handed him the magazine. He glanced at the table of contents. "I don't see her," he said, looking at the names of contributors.

"Oh—Rose Alban was her pen name," Julie said. "She didn't publish under her real name."

"Why not?"

"She told me once she didn't want her old students giggling over her most personal thoughts. I can see her point. It's a small town."

He located Rose Alban's name and flipped to the page listed.

Tears
By Rose Alban

Tears cleanse the soul, they say,
And mine have fallen like April rain.
Surely my soul is shriven clean,
But I would gladly lose it
To be with you again.
Tears ease the heart, they say,
Then, oh! The pain should go away—
I have wept seas of tears for you,
But pain and yearning stay.

He knew nothing about poetry, but this did not strike him as particularly good work. Still, its tone surprised him. "Wow," he said, "this is more passionate than I expected. When'd she publish this?"

"Last year. Do you suppose it's about George?"

"Maybe," he said, keeping his face noncommittal. He didn't want to tell her his ugly little theory that Rebecca might have had more than one man. Julie was in enough pain.

She picked up a dark blue book with an imitation-leather cover. "Look at this," she said, her beautiful face full of sorrow. "It was wrapped up in white paper, with a card that had my name on it. She meant it for my birthday present. She'd written out her poems for me. I can't even bear to look at it, Jake. She couldn't have given me a more personal present."

He sat beside her, picked up the card that said, "To my Darling Niece." He read the verse and Rebecca's neat inscription, "To Julie with all my love, Aunt Rebecca."

"Your birthday isn't for another month," he said.

"I know. She always planned ahead. Look, Jake—she copied all those poems out by hand. Over a hundred of them. It must have taken her weeks."

He took the book and opened it.

His eyes fell on the first poem.

> To Julie, When I Am Gone
>
> When I am gone, dearest, to a better place,
> Do not grieve for me.
> Even on that further shore
> I will have tender thoughts—for thee.
>
> And though we meet no more in this little life,
> I pray to fates above
> That life always brings thee beauty
> And the courage, dear, to love . . .

Jake winced. Rebecca had hit the mark a little too truly; no wonder Julie could not read further. He shut the book and placed it back in her hands, closing her fingers around it. "Don't read it now," he said quietly. "Save it for later."

"It isn't fair," she said, her brown eyes flashing. "Rebecca always loved beauty, but life never gave her anything beautiful. She never, ever hurt anyone. She was a gentle, sensitive soul, and—and—"

"Come on," he said. "Let's get out of here. You've had enough of this for one day. I know that look. Your ideals are outraged, and you'd fight the gods on Olympus itself if they'd condescend to a grudge match."

"I have to put Rebecca's things back," Julie objected. "She'd hate having them strewn all over like this."

"She's not here to hate it," Jake said. "We'll finish tomorrow."

He hadn't meant to be cruel, only honest, but her shoulders sagged as his words struck all the hope out of her. She hugged the closed book to her chest.

"I'm sorry," he said more gently. "I didn't mean it that way. Come on. You haven't eaten all day."

"I'm not hungry."

"You always say that."

He stood and pulled her to her feet. He would have kissed her, but he knew it would be wrong in Rebecca's virginal, deserted bedroom.

Julie didn't speak. She seemed in a sort of daze as she let him lead her from the bedroom back to the living room. He helped her put on her light jacket. She gazed moodily at the dead houseplants in their bone-dry soil. Her eyes moved to the photographs ranged on the piano top again. She stared at them, her face pale.

"Jake," she said in a small voice.

"What?"

"I haven't been in this house much since the funeral— since Rebecca's father died. And I just noticed something."

"What, baby?"

"There are pictures of everyone in the family," she said, nodding toward the piano, "except him. Except her own father. Why?"

An inexplicable chill ran through Jake. He recognized it as the beginning of a dark and dangerous thought that could change everything he thought about the case. It was a thought, for the time being, best kept to himself.

He shook his head, said nothing, and led her out into the darkening evening.

IT WAS AFTER seven o'clock, and both restaurants were locked up tight again. But one of the bars served burgers and pizzas, and Jake yearned for a glass of cold beer.

He and Julie ordered a cheese pizza—she'd always been a purist about pizza and liked it as simple as possible. She nursed a glass of white wine as they sat in a booth, waiting.

The soft click of billiard balls came from the table in the middle of the room, and the jukebox was playing Garth Brooks' rendition of "Nobody Gets Off in This Town."

"Ought to be the official town anthem," Jake muttered and sipped his beer. Julie tried a smile, failed at it and gazed around the smoky room. The bars' patrons seemed mostly old men, dressed in jeans or overalls. They wore ball caps or cowboy hats pulled over their foreheads, and the place was redolent of half a century of their cigarette smoke and beer.

Only a few young men, who seemed like tired laborers, sat silently at the bar, looking bored and depressed, as if they yearned to be elsewhere. They had glanced hungrily at Julie when she walked in the door, but Jake had warned them off with an aggressive glance. They acted now as if she wasn't even among them.

A plump woman with a dirty apron came to the table and set down the pizza, two paper plates, paper napkins and plastic knives and forks. The pizza looked surprisingly good, and Julie was surprised to realize she was ravenous.

"Jake," she said between bites, "I can't get the thought out of my mind—that Rebecca didn't have any pictures of her father anywhere. What do you suppose that means?"

He shrugged carelessly. "It could mean a lot of things. Including that he was always the one who took the pictures. Don't read too much into it."

Julie cocked one eyebrow and gave him a searching look. Once, such an answer would have quieted her. She knew him far better now; he was hiding something from her. She was sure of it.

"You're sitting over there thinking a mile a minute," she said. "I can tell."

He gave her a small but wicked smile. "I'm thinking a mile a minute about you. As usual."

"You're a vile flatterer—as usual. I'm serious. What do you think about Rebecca and her father?"

"I'm serious about you," he said. "Completely. As for Rebecca and her father, what *should* I think about them? I don't know that much. What can you tell me about them?"

Julie looked at him, half in frustration, half in awe. "You're good, you know that?" she said. "I tell you not to flatter me, and you flatter me more. I ask you a question, and you turn it into a question of your own."

"We're not talking about me," he said. "We're talking about Rebecca and her father. Aren't we?"

She sighed and nodded. "Yes. Frankly, I never knew her father that well. While he was alive, Rebecca usually came to see us. Will Albert wasn't invited. My mother didn't like him. We only stopped by Casino a few times when he was alive."

"Why didn't she like him?"

"I told you, she could never accept him as her stepfather. She resented him and thought my grandmother had remarried too fast."

Jake seemed to weigh this. "She remarried too fast. Was that all there was to it?"

Julie searched for a way to put it delicately, but couldn't. "All right," she said. "It makes my mother sound like a snob, but she also thought my grandmother remarried *beneath* herself. Lynn's father was an accountant for the oil company. He had some education, he was artistic and very musical. The piano sitting in Rebecca's house was originally his. My mother says he played it beautifully."

"I see," Jake said. "But Will Albert was different."

Julie looked around the room again. She had seen Will Albert only a few times, but some of these aging men reminded her of him. He'd had a wiry, bent body and a haggard face that looked both suspicious and fierce.

Even when she was a child, she could see he had an imperious nature. He eyed her as if he sensed she was a potential enemy, as if he thought that her heart was full of rebellion and that she would rise up against him if given half a chance.

His voice, when he deigned to talk, was snappish. Lynn said he shaved only twice a week. His fingernails were always black with oil, his cracked hands were dirty and seamed with it, as if the stuff had sunk permanently into his skin.

"Will Albert was different," she agreed, echoing Jake's words. "My grandfather worked in an office. Will worked in the oil fields. He was a mechanic of some sort—I never understood exactly what he did, really."

She gave Jake a sheepish smile. "When I was little, I knew there were two kinds of oil, refined and crude. I asked my mother if there were two kinds of oilmen, too...if my grandfather was refined and Will was crude."

Jake smiled wryly. "What'd she think of that?"

"She thought it was funny. She was very pleased. But that was how she saw the two men, exactly. She said her own father was kind, but Will was demanding and strict. She said he was so strict because he was insecure. He knew he had no right to be in that house. He didn't fit in."

Jake studied her. "Why did your grandmother marry him, do you think?"

Julie thought back to four years ago. She had never seen Will Albert dressed up until he was lying in his coffin, and then she'd been amazed. In repose, his gaunt face had been handsome, almost regal.

"Old devil," was all her mother had muttered when she looked down at him. She'd said it so quietly that only Julie had heard her.

"I have the feeling," Julie said, "that my grandmother was in shock when my grandfather died. There was no warning—none. Then Will Albert came courting. And, well, I also have the feeling that in his prime, he may have been..."

She hesitated. Jake furnished the words for her. "Attractive? Sexy?"

She nodded. "Exactly. In a sort of swaggering way. And my grandmother was still a young woman. Maybe she was lonely. Or maybe frightened of being a widow for the rest of her life. Or maybe both."

Jake signaled for another glass of wine for her, another beer for himself.

"I shouldn't have another," Julie said. "It makes my head feel all fuzzy."

"You need to relax," he said. "Tell me what happened between your mother and Rebecca after your grandmother died. Do you know?"

Julie smoothed back her hair pensively, remembering. "My grandmother was ill for a while, but from what I understood, she never let anyone know *how* ill. She lived to see Rebecca finish college. That was her dream, that both her daughters finish college. She died a month later. I don't think my mother ever respected Rebecca for staying in Casino after her mother's death."

Jake looked dubious. "It was Rebecca's life."

"Yes," Julie answered. "But you have to understand that my mother didn't think it was much of a life. Lynn got out of Casino as fast as she could. She couldn't understand why Rebecca didn't leave, too."

The heavyset waitress put a mug of beer and a glass of white wine before them. Then she placed one hand on her hip. "Do I know you?" she asked, scowling at Julie. "Aren't you Rebecca Albert's niece?"

Startled, Julie looked up at the woman. "Yes. Have we met? I'm sorry I don't remember."

"I saw you at Will's funeral," she said. "I'm Mary Prewitt Horner. My cousin was Annie Prewitt. She and Rebecca grew up next door to each other. Thick as thieves they were."

Jake scrutinized the woman, gave her a friendly smile. "We're in town checking on Rebecca's whereabouts. She disappeared almost eight weeks ago."

The woman grunted and nodded, her face unreadable. "And you're that policeman. From Oklahoma."

Jake's smile stayed cool and winning. "Right. Word gets around fast."

"It's a small town. I heard from Donnie Luffmiller you was here, askin' questions."

"Let me ask you one," Jake said. "What does the town think happened to Rebecca Albert?"

Mary gave a snort and tossed her head. "This country's goin' to the dogs. You wouldn't find me goin' alone to no city, the way Rebecca was always doin'. Why, people'll cut your throat just to steal the shoes you wear."

Julie flinched at the woman's casual, almost callous, assumption that Rebecca had met with violence.

Mary Horner wiped her hand on her smeared apron. "My nephew Norvell, he got beat up with a lead pipe in a parking lot in Fort Worth, and what for? Thirty-four dollars is what. Nossir. Casino may be boring, but you can walk the streets safe."

"You say Rebecca was always going off to the city?" Jake asked. "How often? Which city?"

"Why, Lubbock, of course. She started goin' once a month, then about every two weeks."

"That's interesting, very interesting," Jake said. "That's a long trip for a woman to take alone. Why was she going so often?"

"Chiropractor," Mary said without hesitation. "She threw out her back a few years back, taking care of her daddy. Slipped a disk. Last winter she started limpin' as bad as the old gray mare. I saw her hobblin' down the street one day, and I said to her, 'Rebecca, soon they'll be puttin' you and me out to pasture.'"

"Mrs. Horner," Jake said, giving her his most engaging smile, "can you tell me the name of her chiropractor?"

"I don't recall she ever said. I don't hold with chiropractors myself. But there's them that swears by 'em. Still, me myself, I wouldn't go clear into Lubbock for one. But Rebecca, her daddy always swore by the chiropractor."

Jake lowered his voice. "I heard she may have had a gentleman friend in Austin. Do you think there's any truth to that?"

Mary snorted again and wiped the back of her hand over her double chin. "A fancy man? That's Charity Klopp's talk. I don't believe anything that one says. She's gone through more than one pink-elephant phase, if you get my meaning."

Jake nodded. "I get your meaning. So you don't think Rebecca had a boyfriend? Ever?"

"Oh, there's *stories*," the woman said scornfully. "That she had one years and years ago, but that her daddy put the kibosh on that. But if you believe every story that's ever been told in this town, you wouldn't have room for a single fact. No, she never had a boyfriend I knew of. She was too shy and caught up in her own imagination, her poetry and her storybooks."

Julie frowned in puzzlement. "Storybooks?" she said, thinking of children's picture books.

"You know what I mean," Mary said. "Novels. Storybooks. Rebecca kind of lived in her own world. Always did. Even when she was a little kid."

"Really?" Jake said. "How do you mean? Could you sit down with us, Mrs. Horner? I could buy you a beer, or a glass of wine."

The woman smiled with obvious pleasure. She gave Jake an almost flirtatious look. "Me? No, I gotta handle all these old wildcatters alone tonight. My husband's home with a migraine. I've about run my legs off."

"Too bad," Jake said and seemed genuinely regretful. "But you were saying Rebecca lived in her own world. Even as a child...?"

"Well, I'm younger than she and Annie were. But my mama used to send me over there to play. I could never figure out what they were playin'. It was always pretend games. I never had much use for them. I'd play marbles with the Roush boys, who lived across the street, or baseball or tag or spit in the ocean. You know—real games."

"What sort of pretend games?" Jake asked.

Mary put both hands on her hips and gave another snort. "Well, the summer I remember best, they was both playing they was queen of the jungle. It was out of some comic book or something. They'd climb up on my aunt's back porch and pretend it was a tree house. Then they swung on ropes and pretended they was vines."

She laughed. "Rebecca undid her pigtails so her hair hung down her back like a wild woman. She and Annie carried butter knives in the belts of their shorts and pretended they was daggers. And they'd fight imaginary snakes and tigers and Lord knows what nonsense. They looked ridiculous, and the Roush boys used to tease them, but Annie and Rebecca, they paid no nevermind."

Julie was surprised and rather charmed. Rebecca swinging on ropes and pretending to be queen of the jungle? This was a side of her aunt that she'd never known.

"Imaginative kids, eh?" Jake said, encouraging the woman's remembrance. "Did it wear off when they got older? It usually does. When they discovered boys."

"Oh, they didn't discover boys," Mary said with a shake of her head. "That would have been too ordinary. They discovered movie stars. Rebecca's daddy wouldn't let her pin up all those pictures on her wall, but my aunt didn't mind. Oh, yes. I was twelve years old and already kissin' real boys. But Rebecca and Annie didn't do anything but sit around and moon over Hollywood actors. No, I don't think Rebecca ever had one real date in high school. Nor Annie neither."

"But Annie married," Jake said. "Didn't she?"

Mary rolled her eyes comically. "She went off to college and met a real live feller. She found out there's some things a girl can't get from movies."

Jake rewarded her with a knowing smile, then sobered. "But Annie—your cousin—she's passed away now, hasn't she?"

Mary's face sombered, too. "Just a few months back. Right after Christmas. Seems like just yesterday they was swinging off Aunt Mott's back porch and yelling about— what's them big snakes?—pylons?"

"Pythons," Jake said.

"Yeah," Mary said and sighed. "Pythons."

"Mary!" A man's voice, elderly, irritable, raised itself above the desultory buzz of background conversation and the twanging guitars of the jukebox. "Mary? What's a man have to do to get another round of beers around here? Get a court order?"

"Duty calls," Mary said, the animation dying from her face. She spoke to Jake, ignoring Julie. "You come back tomorrow afternoon and talk to me, when it's not so crowded. I'll see what else I remember."

Julie said, "I'm sorry your cousin passed away."

"Thanks," Mary said mechanically and walked off, her tread heavy.

Jake looked at her, his eyebrow cocked. "Rebecca sounds like a creative kid. Maybe even had a little hell in her. What do you suppose happened?"

"Ask your new girlfriend," Julie said with a brusque nod in Mary Horner's direction.

But Jake didn't laugh. His expression grew serious again. "I mean it, Jules. What happened to that little girl who wanted to be queen of the jungle and kill pythons with a butter knife? The idealistic teenager who was in love with movie stars?"

Julie looked around the cheerless, smoky room again, feeling oppressed by it. "I don't know," she said. "What bothers me is what she said about Charity Klopp. Do you believe her? That Charity can't be trusted?"

"No," Jake said. "I think Charity told us exactly what Rebecca said to her."

Julie didn't know which was worse, suspecting the mysterious George O'Keefe of every sort of villainy, or having no leads whatsoever. "Then O'Keefe does exist?" she asked. "And he did take money from Rebecca?"

"All the evidence points to it," he said.

She shook her head and pushed away her wine, untouched. "I want to get out of here, Jake. It seems the deeper we dig, the less we know. Let's go—please."

He nodded, and she shrugged into her jacket, which had been draped around her shoulders. She felt suddenly cold and shaky, and with unsteady fingers she buttoned it to her chin.

Jake rose, put on his jacket and helped her to her feet. He threw some bills on the table and walked her out the door.

Outside, the night was surprisingly chilly, moonless, starless, and only the town's few street lamps lit the darkness. The cold, smokeless air struck her as smartly as a slap, making her cheeks sting. Greedily, she drew it into her lungs, but it was so clean and icy it made her feel dizzy.

They walked down the broken sidewalk to where her car was parked. "Do you want me to drive?" he asked quietly.

She nodded, swayed a little.

"Are you all right?" he asked, catching her by the lapels of her jacket and staring into her eyes.

She gazed up at him, his handsome features half illuminated by the dim light, half lost in shadow. She sagged against him, her hands gripping his shoulders.

He bent nearer to her, his body tense, one arm going around her waist. "Jules—sugar. What's wrong?"

She didn't know if the long, grueling day had drained her of all character, or if it had simply killed any hypocrisy. She was full of naked, shivery need of him.

"Don't leave me alone tonight, Jake," she whispered. "I don't want to be alone. Please . . ."

He bent nearer still, and she could feel the warmth of his lips almost touching hers. "Julie . . ."

She shook her head helplessly. "I need you tonight. I want you. It's not the same as loving you. It's selfish, I know. I won't lie about it."

She thought he was going to kiss her, but he didn't. When he spoke, his voice was harder. "No. It's not the same as loving. But sometimes sex is enough. I won't lie, either."

For a charged moment they stared at each other, their warm breath mingling on the cool air.

She whispered, "Today I've seen you charm three different women to get what you want. You did it in English, you did it in French, you did it in Spanish. And you played Donnie Luffmiller like he was a flute."

"I did it for you," he said.

She knew this was true, yet she thought of him doing this same thing with far more dangerous people, with thieves and drug dealers and prostitutes and junkies. She thought of Billy Cable, dead before his twenty-first birthday.

"It scares me," she breathed. "It scares me to death."

"It's what I do," he said.

Her heart beat so hard she could hear it in her ears. *I want you*, it seemed to say. *I want you. I want you.*

He gave her a bitter little smile. "Back to square one, are we, Julie?"

9

NERVOUSLY, SHE UNLOCKED the door and stepped inside, flicking on the light. She turned and looked, half-fearful, half-expectantly at Jake.

"Do you still want me to come inside?" he asked.

She heard the double entendre vibrating in his words, but she thought, *I won't play games.*

She raised her chin almost defiantly. "Yes," she said, her cheeks heating. "I do."

He gave a cynical little nod and stepped in beside her, pulling the door shut. The automatic lock clicked, and he slid the dead bolt into place.

Wordlessly, he took off her coat and hung it on a hanger in the closet. Then he stripped off his jacket and hung it next to her coat.

He turned to her, gave her a sideways smile. "How do you want it done, Julie? Fast? Or slow? Tough? Or tender? What scenario do you have in mind?"

Her cheeks burned more hotly. "I don't have any scenario in mind. I just wanted to be close to you, and I thought you wanted to be close to me."

He reached to the top button of her blouse, undid it slowly and carefully. "There are many ways to be close. Many."

He undid the second button, then the third. He took the lapels of her shirt and parted them lazily. He stared at her breasts, which swelled up roundly over the edges of their lacy cups. He drew her close and she did not resist.

He bent low, placing his lips against the shadowy valley between her breasts. Her own flesh was cool, but his mouth was hot as a brand. She shuddered involuntarily.

He straightened again so that he towered over her. With leisurely movements, he finished unbuttoning her blouse. "Last night I ripped your clothes off," he said, his voice almost a purr. "How about tonight I take it nice and slow?"

She swallowed hard, but she met his eyes. "We both tore our clothes off. It wasn't all your doing. It was mine, too. Jake, I've hurt your feelings. I didn't mean to."

"Forget emotions," he said. "Isn't that what you want—somebody to help you forget?" He eased her blouse from her shoulders, guided it down her arms and let it fall softly to the floor. He reached to the waistband of her jeans, unsnapped them. He kept his eyes on her.

Her body throbbed with desire, but he was making things go wrong somehow; there was coldness, almost cruelty, in the way he touched her, undressed her.

"All right," she said, tears of exasperation rising in her eyes. "You think I'm only using you. You're angry. You want me to feel cheap."

"Feel however you want to feel about it," he said, unzipping her jeans.

"Dammit, Jake!" she said angrily. She pushed away from him with both hands. She fastened the snap at the waistband of her jeans and glared up at him. "I'm sorry I hurt you. It's not as if I don't care for you. I do. I always have."

"Thanks. I love you, too. Now—you want to screw or not?"

"No, I don't," she retorted. "I never wanted to 'screw' with you. I always thought what we did was making love."

"I always did, too."

She walked to the door of the bathroom, leaned her head against the chipped door frame. She closed her eyes. "I didn't ask you here tonight just because I wanted a man. I wanted you. Only you."

He said nothing. She was conscious that she was half-undressed before him, but she didn't care. Her emotions felt far more naked and vulnerable than her body.

She squeezed her eyes shut more tightly, and the familiar painful knot was back in her throat, making it hard for her to talk.

"You want the truth?" she asked. "You're the only man I've ever wanted this way. I never *understood* sex until I met you. It was awkward and sweaty and embarrassing and stupid. Men wanted it, but I didn't. I thought I would never enjoy it. What a laugh."

"I'm not laughing," he said. She could feel his eyes on her, sense the tension in the air between them.

"All right," she said wearily. "After I left you, I hoped I could find somebody else. I wanted to, somebody tamer, somebody committed, who didn't love danger more than he did me. But I've only been with one other man since then. Just once. And I felt nothing. Except—a kind of weird despair. I kept wondering if I should try again."

She opened her eyes and turned to face him, leaning against the wall and crossing her arms over her breasts.

His face was rigidly controlled, as if he was fighting pain and didn't want her to know. "Julie," he said from the corner of his mouth, "do you always have to be so damned honest?"

"Yes," she said. "And you know it. It's not that I don't care for you, Jake. It's that I don't love you enough to share you with your job. Maybe I'm too selfish. Maybe too immature. Or too weak. But I can't do it. And you'll never change—will you?"

"I might," he said, muscles knotting in his jaw. "I might change. If you'd give it a chance."

"No," she said sadly. "You won't. And it's wrong of me to want you to. But I did love you, Jake. I suppose I still do. In my way. But my way just isn't good enough."

Something fleeting passed in his eyes. He swallowed, bent, swept up her shirt and held it clenched in his hand. "I'm sorry I taunted you," he said. "I love you, too. Maybe my way isn't good enough, either." He took a step toward her, holding out her blouse. "Here, sugar. You want your shirt back?"

She smiled at him, and felt tears bite her eyes. "No," she said. "That's what I've been trying to say to you with all these words, I don't mind being naked with you. It's never felt wrong."

She saw him catch his breath as she reached behind her back and unsnapped her bra. She slid off the undergarment and dropped it. Then she held out her arms to him.

He stepped to her, pulling her into his arms almost roughly. He brought his lips down on hers with such devouring passion he made her gasp.

His throat was tight with longing, and lust seemed to have thickened his blood; his heart slammed crazily to drive it through his body.

He tried not to think of the past or future, only of *now*. And now Julie's mouth was warm, pliant and responsive beneath his own. His tongue tasted hers, and his hands cupped the maddening sweetness of her breasts.

He ran his thumbs over her nipples, feeling them tighten into inviting little points, and his groin swelled and tightened in response.

Drunk with needing her, wanting her to need him, he maneuvered her to the edge of the bed. He sat down, pulling her standing body between his legs. With his mouth, he made love to one taut breast, then the other.

He knew how to start slowly, almost teasingly, the pressure of lips whisper soft, barely touching, his tongue caressing her as if she were a rare delicacy he meant to make last as long as possible.

He knew how to raise the tension in her, slowly, but with an inevitability that would make her body yearn, he prayed, as much as his did.

He kissed and wooed her sensitive flesh with more fervor, more intensity, until her body quivered, and she began to move her head in dreamy circles, so her long hair swept him like silk.

She made little, kittenlike sounds of pleasure and her hands tightened on his shoulders. His mouth moved down the velvet softness of her flat stomach.

He unfastened her jeans again, his mouth moving lower, lower. He loved every inch of her, loved kissing her all over, loved making her forget everything except her body and his, making their own separate universe of dizzying need and fulfillment.

"Oh, Jake," she said with a little moan of pleasurable pain. He tried to hold her in place, to keep exploring and treasuring her, but she sank to her knees before him, her brown eyes languorous and heavy-lidded with desire.

She gave him a tremulous smile that made his heart turn over in his chest. She reached up and began to unbutton his shirt.

When it was undone, she pushed it open and began to stroke his chest. Then she leaned forward and kissed him where she always did in the shower, on the breastbone, a long, seductive kiss that almost cut off his breathing.

"Julie," he groaned, warning in his voice, but she was unzipping his jeans. Her small hand tightened around him with a firm yet delicate touch that sent shudders through him.

He rose from the bed, drawing her up with him. He kicked off his boots. She kicked off her shoes. He practically wrenched off his jeans and flung them away. She stepped out of hers, so that her jeans and panties lay around her naked feet like a little pool of white lace and denim.

He picked her up, and she wound her arms around his neck, snuggling against him and kissing his breastbone again.

He sank to the bed with her, and she opened herself to him like a flower. He lost all rational thought and became one with her, moving in unison, thrusting back and forth, riding out the long, sweet, powerful storm of their desire.

Afterward, spent and warm, they nuzzled together until they dozed. He awoke when she squirmed, as always, from his arms. With a little sigh that sounded sad, she rolled over, grasping the pillow and burrowing her cheek into it.

She lay with her back to him. He felt a fatalistic symbolism in her movement. As before, he had possessed her only temporarily. He could not hold her.

She would slip away from him again. She loved him—in her way. But not enough. And how had he always loved her? Too possessively, too arrogantly? With too little understanding and too much pride?

She was right about him, always had been. He had meant to make her his wife, but keep danger as his mistress. He had expected Julie, not himself, to bend and change.

The wives of other cops smiled and pretended harm could never touch their men; that's how they got through life. He'd wanted her to do the same. But Julie was constitutionally incapable of such pretense.

She was honest to a fault, and her honesty told her that her future with him was neither safe nor clear. When this interlude was over, whether Rebecca was found or not, he would go back to Tulsa, and she would go back to the Texas hill country.

He'd chase criminals in the city. She'd paint flowers in the country. She'd said she'd been looking for someone tamer, more committed. Jake feared she'd find the son of a bitch.

He imagined her pregnant with another man's child, and it made him almost physically ill. He reached for her and pulled her to him, held her tightly in his arms, his cheek resting against her silky, tumbled hair.

She came to him without protest, making a sleepy little murmur. She nestled against him with a sigh and was deep asleep again, her breathing soft and regular, her hand resting lightly on his arm.

But before her closeness could drive off his troubling thoughts, she stretched and struggled out of his embrace, rolling over and clutching the pillow again, snuggling into it and her own private world.

JULIE PUT Rebecca's possessions back into the closet, trying to arrange them as neatly as Rebecca had. Jake was in Rebecca's little guest room, which had seldom had any guests. Julie had stayed in it precisely three times after Will Albert's death. She knew of no one else who had.

She went through Rebecca's bureau drawers and found nothing strange or suspicious. Rebecca's humble lingerie and modest sweaters were arranged in almost regimental order. A bottom drawer held five pastel nightgowns, still folded up in their plastic bags.

Julie gazed down at them with a strange stab of guilt. Almost every year for Rebecca's birthday, her mother sent Rebecca a nightgown or a set of bubble bath and dusting powder. "She's so hard to buy for," Lynn always grumbled.

Two of the bath sets were still in their gift boxes and had been put away in the closet. The nightgowns had never been worn. Lynn's gifts to Rebecca had been useless and repetitive. If Rebecca had stayed in this house and lived to be eighty, would her bureau have overflowed with too many nightgowns to wear, would her closet have burst with more bath sets than one woman could use?

Julie sighed and stood up. She went down the hall to the guest bedroom. The room had once been Will's, but after his death, Rebecca had moved out the old four-poster bed and bulky matching dresser and bureau. She'd made the room not only into a guest room but a sort of mini-library and auxiliary study.

Jake sat on the double bed, sorting through a stack of photographs and scrapbooks. He wore a turquoise shirt of western cut, which set off his bronzed complexion and black hair. He looked so handsome that her heart stopped for a painful moment.

Handsome is as handsome does, she told herself, and tried not to think about last night. Would she make love with him again tonight? Of course she would.

But when it was time for him to go back to Oklahoma, she would tell him goodbye again. There was no future in this mutual obsession. Better to part quickly and cleanly when the time came, than let the relationship drag on, degenerate once more into arguments and bitterness.

"Find anything?" she asked with false cheeriness, leaning against the door frame.

He gave her a sardonic glance and then nodded at an open photograph album in his lap. "Rebecca must have kept every photograph and greeting card that came her way."

Julie smiled in affectionate remembrance. "You're right. She did."

"This one," he said with a disgusted nod at the opened album, "is full of nothing but class pictures. Every class she taught. All dated. All the names written underneath."

"She taught almost thirty years, you know."

"That's a lot of noses to wipe and galoshes to help put on. Who are these Mexican kids? I haven't seen any Mexicans in town."

Julie walked to his side and stared down at the book. "The children of oil-field workers, mostly. They moved on when the wells played out, I guess."

Jake turned the page and narrowed his eyes. "Here's a couple of Indian kids—twins."

"Oh," Julie said, nodding. "The Sutton twins. They went on to the University of Texas and played football. They were both All-Americans. One's a coach now, and one teaches science at Baylor."

He raised one eyebrow. "Sounds like she kept track of them."

"She did. They were favorites of hers. I think all the minority kids were. She had a soft spot for them. I gave her a little ceramic statue once, of a little Mexican girl holding a kitten."

She looked at the bookshelf. "There it is," she said with a smile. She moved to the shelves and picked it up.

She turned it in her fingers, studying it. "I bought her this when I was nine years old. I only had a dollar to spend. Imagine her keeping it all these years."

She set the statuette down and turned back to Jake. "She kept all the cards I made her, too. In a special scrapbook. She made such a fuss over how wonderful my drawings were that I never *bought* her a card in my life—Christmas, birthday, Valentine, anything. I always made them."

Jake frowned. He stared at her in silence for so long that the back of her neck grew prickly.

"What's wrong?" she asked.

"They're not here. Not one," he said. "There's no scrapbook of your cards."

She smiled because he had to be mistaken. "But there *is*, Jake. I've seen it. Every time I came, she brought it out and we had to look at it. I remember being embarrassed by the scrawls I thought were so beautiful when I was little . . ."

"There's no such book here," he said, his gaze not wavering from hers.

"There has to be. It's a big blue book, almost the color of your shirt. The kind you can add pages to. She kept my birthday photos in it, too, back to my really first birthday, the day I was born."

"Julie, no such book is here," he repeated. "Not in her closet, not on the shelves with these others, not in her desk. It's not in the bedroom, is it?"

"Of course not," she said, puzzled and dismayed. "I would have recognized it. You must be wrong. It's with these others. Maybe she put it in a different cover."

She sat beside him and began fanning through the books. He was right. There were books devoted to Rebecca's pupils, to family photos, to church events, to clippings from the county newspaper, to Christmas cards, to birthday cards, Dear Teacher cards and miscellaneous cards. But there were none of Julie's drawings and birthday snapshots.

"I don't understand this," she said, shaking her head. She raised her eyes to his. "Why would it be gone?"

Twin frown lines appeared between his eyebrows. "I don't know. There are other things that aren't here, either. Mary Horner said Rebecca had been going to a chiropractor in Austin for two years. But there are no chiropractor bills. Not a single one."

"Maybe she paid cash," Julie suggested.

"Maybe she did," he said, the frown lines deepening. "But I can't find any receipts, either. Wouldn't she have wanted them for her tax statements? For insurance benefits?"

Julie's mouth had gone peculiarly dry. She made a futile little gesture with her hands. "*Can* you claim chiropractor bills? *Will* insurance reimburse you?"

"That's something I'll have to check. In the meantime, here's something you should look at. I haven't opened it, it's not my place to."

He picked up a long yellow envelope, put it in her hand. On its front was clearly written, "Last Will and Testament, Rebecca Ann Albert."

The words *Last Will and Testament* had such a final, funereal ring to them that Julie felt as if she'd been struck in the stomach.

"Oh," she said in a small voice. The envelope was not sealed. She opened it and drew out a sheaf of folded papers. Her vision blurred as she skimmed through them.

"She's leaving all her physical property to Mama—to Lynn," Julie said and swallowed. "The house, the furniture, her car . . . except her books and poetry. Those she leaves to me. She wants whatever money is left to be split between the church and her school."

She lowered the papers to her lap, her hand shaking. "Where'd you find this?" she asked.

"In this desk," he said, nodding toward it. "All alone in the middle drawer. Like that's its special place. Or like—"

He didn't finish the sentence. "Or like what?" Julie asked.

He hesitated, shrugged. "Like she wanted it to be found easily in case it was necessary. That means nothing. Lots of people do that."

"I don't *want* it to be necessary," Julie said with passion, her voice choked.

Jake took her in his arms and pulled her close. "Hey," he said, "hang in there. It's only a few pieces of paper. It doesn't prove she's dead. It doesn't prove anything."

She buried her face against the hardness of his shoulder, grateful for his words. "I'm glad you're here, Jake."

He said nothing, only stroked her hair.

THEY PUT Rebecca's possessions back in place and closed the house again.

"I want to talk to the principal of her school," Jake said. "Then go back and talk to Mary Horner again."

He tossed her a teasing glance. "Think you can keep your jealousy in check?"

She locked the outer door and gave him a rueful smile. "I'll try. And shouldn't we call Donnie Luffmiller? To see if the police have tracked down George O'Keefe?"

He nodded. He put his hand on the small of her back and guided her down the porch stairs. "I don't suppose it would do any good to talk to the neighbors?"

She shook her head. "The police already did. It was the same old story. They noticed nothing out of the ordinary."

"The Prewitts don't live next door anymore?"

"They've been gone for years. Annie's father ran the dime store. It closed down years ago. He got another job in Lubbock. Her folks moved there."

"When was that?" he asked, opening the car door for her.

"Years ago, if I remember. Once, Rebecca said that Annie was afraid her folks wouldn't have enough money for a church wedding like she wanted. Because the dime store was closing. But her grandparents paid for it, and her mother made all the gowns . . ."

Jake got into the car beside her, started the engine and headed toward the school.

"Mrs. Prewitt made Rebecca's bridesmaid dress," she said. "I can remember Rebecca telling me how she dieted and dieted so she could wear a size smaller than usual. It was probably the most beautiful dress she ever owned. It's still in her closet in a plastic bag. She could never bear to part with it, even though she said she'd never fit in it again. Oh, Jake, I'm babbling. I'm sorry."

"It's okay, sugar," he said. He knew she was nervous and worn-out. Finding the will had shaken her.

He parked in front of the school yard and walked Julie inside. The day was overcast, with something between a drizzle and a mist, and no children played outside.

Up close, the brick building was more decrepit than he'd thought at first glance, the mortar crumbling and shot through with jagged cracks.

Inside, the place had a close, mildewy smell, as if the furnace blasted too hotly all winter long and the roof or the plumbing leaked. There was also an odor of chicken noodle soup and hot dogs drifting from the second floor. The cafeteria was probably gearing up for lunch hour. A large, faded print of George Washington hung in the lobby in a large, tarnished frame. It looked so old that George might have hung it there himself.

From down the hall came the sound of childish voices singing, "Merrily We Row Our Boat." The principal's office was directly to the left, its pebbled glass window labeled with chipping black paint.

Jake ushered Julie inside and nodded in greeting to a woman who sat at a desk, hammering out some sort of report on an ancient electric typewriter. She wore a blue pantsuit and had rhinestones edging her eyeglasses. A sign on her desk said, Mrs. Phipping, School Secretary.

Jake pulled out his badge and showed it to her. "Mrs. Phipping, I'm Jake Good Thunder of the Oklahoma State Police, and this is Miss Julie FitzJames, the niece of Rebecca Albert. We'd like to ask Mrs. Cummings a few questions."

Mrs. Phipping cringed at the sight of the badge. She jumped up from her desk and pounded on a closed door. "Mrs. Cummings," she said rather desperately. "Police are here about Miss Albert."

"Tell them to come in," called a voice.

"Go in," Mrs. Phipping said, practically hugging the wall. "Have you found her?" she asked Jake. "Is she— dead?"

Jake shook his head. "We're just making inquiries, ma'am."

He opened the door and let Julie enter first. The woman behind the desk stood and gave them a solemn nod of greeting. "I'm Tammy Cummings, the principal," she said.

Jake showed his badge again, introduced himself and Julie. Mrs. Cummings invited them to sit and took her own chair again. She was a chubby young woman with a round, earnest face and blond hair.

Her answers to Jake's questions were clear and thoughtful. She knew nothing about Rebecca's disappearance. It had come as a great shock to the staff and to herself, and no, nothing in Rebecca's demeanor had given any hint of what might have happened to her.

"Did she seem happy with her work, her students?" Jake asked.

Mrs. Cummings put her elbows on her desk, clasped her hands together and looked at Jake. "Frankly, Mr. Good Thunder, none of us have been completely happy in our work. There's talk of closing the school down, of consolidating with the Windemere system. This could be our school's last year."

Jake frowned, wondering why Julie hadn't mentioned this back before. He stole a glance at her and saw she was as surprised as he was.

"Oh, it won't come to a vote until summer," Mrs. Cummings said. "But the handwriting's on the wall. The population's shrunk. We've lost our tax base. The building's a disaster, but there's no money to fix it. And we no longer have the students to fill it."

"But my aunt never said a word about this," Julie said, clutching the edge of the principal's desk. "She must have been worried to death. She's taught here all her life."

"We've all known it was coming," Mrs. Cummings said philosophically.

"But what would have happened to Rebecca's job?" Julie asked. "Would she lose it?"

Mrs. Cummings shook her head. "I don't *think* so. But there's a possibility. All of us have the feeling that our fates are a bit up in the air. Did Rebecca seem worried? Yes, but no more or less than the rest of us. She sometimes spoke of taking an early retirement."

"What about her students?" Jake asked, his eyes narrowed. "Did she like them?"

"She always liked them," Mrs. Cummings said with conviction. "But this year she had the smallest class of her career. Only nine. And two are leaving at the end of this month. The Mulcahey family and the Loudermilks are moving to Lubbock. There are still jobs in Lubbock, and families have to go where the jobs are."

"A-are her students upset over her disappearance?" Julie asked. She hated to think of the children being fearful or sad.

"They're taking it well. Of course, we're lucky to have Mrs. Tandy, who's a wonderful substitute and very, very good at answering their questions and assuaging their worries. They already knew her because Rebecca had the flu last fall."

"I—I never heard Rebecca mention a Mrs. Tandy," Julie said, still looking stunned.

"She was recently widowed and moved back to Casino to live with her mother. She was one of Rebecca's students herself. Antoinette Kelly was her maiden name. A very capable young woman."

"I suppose police have gone over Rebecca's personal effects here at the school," Jake said.

Mrs. Cummings nodded. "Rebecca's desk was in apple-pie order, as usual. All her records were neatly organized, nothing missing, nothing out of place."

"That's Rebecca," Julie said, trying to smile. But the smile failed, and her voice sounded unsteady.

Mrs. Cummings gave her a sympathetic look. "She left a few things in the teachers' break room, an umbrella, some rain boots, a plastic raincoat, an extra sweater. The police have already seen them. Would you like to take them home, Miss FitzJames?"

Julie nodded, looking even more stricken.

"I'll get them," the woman said in a kindly voice.

She went to her closet, opened it and drew out a sturdy brown paper box. She came back and handed the carton to Julie, who stared down numbly at her aunt's empty rubber rain boots, black and shiny, with imitation black fur trimming the tops.

Mrs. Cummings sat at her desk again, and Jake said, "Ma'am, just a few more questions. How long did you know Rebecca Albert?"

"Two years. I came when the former principal retired. I knew then, of course, that the job might not be permanent. But my husband had to move back to this area. His father has a ranch he can no longer run alone."

"I see," Jake said. "And the former principal?"

"Retired to the coast. Down around Galveston, I think."

"And you'd noticed nothing out of the ordinary in Rebecca's mood or demeanor this last year?"

"Well," Mrs. Cummings said, "her back seemed to bother her a lot. Her limp was noticeably worse this winter."

"She was seeing a chiropractor in Lubbock?"

"Yes. Fairly regularly."

"Do you know the name?"

"She never mentioned it, to my recollection."

"And other than her back problems?"

"Nothing extraordinary," the woman said with a sigh. "She was disturbed at the first of the year because a good friend had passed away after a long illness, someone who lived in a foreign country, I believe. Australia, I think."

"Annie Prewitt?" Jake offered. "From New Zealand?"

"That's it," Mrs. Cummings agreed. "Yes. I remember she said, 'All my old friends are gone now.' She said it very matter-of-factly. She wasn't one to pity herself or complain."

"But she had friends on the faculty?" Jake asked. "People she'd taught with for years?"

Mrs. Cummings shook her head. "No. The school is like the town, Mr. Good Thunder. It's fading away. Teachers leave if they get a chance. There are few old-timers left. I'm told Rebecca had two close friends, but—"

She paused and shook her head sadly. "But her best friend, Naomi Griswold, died two and a half years ago. And the other, Georgia Fitch, has Alzheimer's, I'm sorry to say. She's had it for almost three years. She's with her son in Odessa."

Julie, never able to disguise her emotions, looked so grieved that Jake wished he could dump the damn box of empty rainwear into the trash, pick her up and carry her off to some Valhalla where sorrow could never touch her again. If he could give her Rebecca, alive and well, so much the better.

But he had more questions to ask, painful ones. "We've been told Rebecca may have been seeing a man in Lubbock. Were you aware of any such relationship?"

Tammy Cummings's round face took on an almost severe look. "I am aware," she said emphatically, "that a sordid story to that effect is starting to make the rounds. And I most certainly *don't* believe it. Neither do any of the teaching staff."

"And what about the fact she lost some money in the last few years—a considerable amount? Did she ever mention that?"

Mrs. Cummings's chin went up as if she disdained the question. "Rebecca was one of those people who never discussed politics, religion or money. She didn't consider such conversation polite."

"Mrs. Cummings," Julie said, holding the brown box as if it held the crown jewels, "what do the children think happened to Rebecca?"

Tammy Cummings allowed herself a dubious smirk. "The favorite theory is that she got hit on the head and lost her memory. The Roush children, however, are hoping that she was kidnapped by a flying saucer. They're still waiting for it to come back for the rest of the staff."

Jake grinned at her and even Julie managed a small smile.

Outside the principal's office, they heard the sound of children singing again, this time about the itsy-bitsy spider who climbed the waterspout.

Julie went so pale, Jake feared she was going to faint. "Rebecca taught me that song and how to play it on the piano when I was five years old," she said. "I bet those are *her* children singing now."

Julie's eyes glistened too brightly, and she thrust the box of Rebecca's belongings at Jake. "Please—hold this a minute?" she begged. "I see a rest room down the hall. I'm sorry, but I feel a little weepy, and I'd rather let it out alone."

Jake nodded grimly. He knew how she hated crying in front of anybody. And he knew, somehow, that this aging, neglected building, where Rebecca had spent so much of her time and given so much of her love, oppressed Julie in a more profound way than her aunt's house had. Hell, it even oppressed him. And the children's piping voices added a poignancy that touched him in spite of himself.

Idly, Jake picked up one of Rebecca's cheap rain boots and began to examine it. It was ankle-high, low-heeled and small—Rebecca must have had tiny feet. He put it back in the box and picked up the other, tilted it toward the glass doors to get more light, and studied it.

He thought he noticed something odd, and examined the boot more closely. When he did, his heart took an excited leap, the same sort of wild, exultant leap it made when he was undercover and was about to make a major bust.

All his senses went on alert, and his skin tingled as if a cold wind had risen.

Suddenly, he had a far better idea of what really happened to Rebecca Albert.

10

ONCE JULIE HAD GIVEN in to the tears that had been threatening all day, she washed her face, and dried it with a rough brown paper towel. She looked at herself in the mirror, squared her shoulders and muttered, "Shape up."

She joined Jake in the lobby. His handsome face had its familiar carefully controlled expression, but she thought it was perhaps *too* carefully controlled. Something was on his mind.

She took his arm, looking up at him. "What is it? Did Mrs. Cummings say something important that I didn't get? You're thinking a mile a minute again, I can tell."

He shook his head and led her out the door. "It's nothing. Let's go back to the house. I want to check something."

Curiosity tingled through her. "Check what?"

He gave her a crooked half smile. "It's nothing. I don't want to get your hopes up—or mine. A case like this, you get a hundred false hunches for every true one."

She got into the car and settled back against the seat in resignation. If Jake didn't intend to talk, he wouldn't. That was Jake.

They drove back to Rebecca's house. She unlocked the door, and once inside, Jake said, "Is her phone still connected?"

Julie nodded. All the utilities were paid up for another month.

"Good," Jake said. "I want you to call Donnie Luffmiller. See if there's been any word from the state police on George O'Keefe."

"Me?" Julie said in surprise. "You're the policeman. Why would he tell me?"

He bent and kissed her on the nose. "Because you're the one with the Bambi-eyes and killer body. His professional impulse would be to stonewall me. But you, he wants to impress. Let him. Flirt with him."

"But—"

"Flirt," Jake said firmly. "And remember, honey catches more flies than vinegar. Here's the phone book. Go get him."

She took the book from him. "But," she said in confusion, "what are you going to do?"

"Check a few things in Rebecca's bedroom. I never looked it over for myself."

"Check *what* things?"

"It may be nothing."

She unbuttoned her jacket and sat down at the desk in frustration. She found the number of the sheriff's office and dialed it. She was put on hold for almost five minutes, listening to a bad recording of patriotic marches that set her teeth on edge.

When Donnie Luffmiller finally lifted the receiver and said hello, she was surprised by the deepness of his voice. With his orange hair, cowlick, jug ears and boyish face, she hadn't noticed he had a deep, resonant voice.

She did just as Jake asked, although she found it distasteful. She was all honey and sugar, all "Oh-can't-you-help-little-old-me, you big strong man?"

He answered her questions at length, at too great a length, as if he was trying to draw out the conversation.

"This is confidential," he told her three times. "This is for your ears only," he told her twice.

He rambled on in minute detail, his tone self-important. "I'll probably know more by this evening," he finished. "The state police are keeping in close touch with me. After all, the woman lived in my jurisdiction. I expect some important calls this afternoon. The FBI is going to be in touch with me, too."

"The FBI," Julie said in manufactured awe. "My *goodness*."

"You want the inside story," Luffmiller intoned, "you stick with me. Outsiders, like this Oklahoman? Nobody's gonna tell him anything. He's playin' private eye, but don't be fooled. You want to find your aunt, you stick with a man from her own hometown. Who's gonna understand the case better? Yes, ma'am, a hometown man, that's what you want."

"I can see that," Julie said. "Oh, yes."

"If you were to have supper with me tonight," Luffmiller said, "I could tell you certain other secret aspects of this case known only to a few insiders. Of course, I'm not talking in front of that Indian individual from Oklahoma. No, ma'am, I will not do that. It isn't his business. I'm too professional for that. But as a personal favor to you—"

Julie hated playing his game, but she forced herself to continue. From between clenched teeth, she said, "Oh, wow, that really puts me in a pickle. I mean, Good Thunder's an old family friend of—my brother's. He and my brother were—roommates. For four years. I'll have to see what I can do. I'll get back in touch with you. All right?"

"He may think he can help you, ma'am, but he flat-out can't," said Luffmiller. "What you want is a man from this town, who knows the background of this case like the palm of his hand."

She took a deep breath, and tried to sound flirtatiously eager. "I'll be back in touch as soon as I can," she promised. *Like hell.*

"Goodby-y-ye," she purred. *Good riddance*, she thought, slamming down the receiver. She sat for a moment, breathing hard and fuming. How dare Luffmiller call Jake "that Indian individual from Oklahoma" in that sneering, dismissive way? Jake had more brains in his little finger than Luffmiller had in his whole carrot-topped head.

Jake appeared in the hall doorway, an ancient valise in his hand. Julie recognized the valise as the one Rebecca had taken off to college and carried for years afterward. It still bore a faded old University of Texas sticker.

"What's in the valise?" she asked.

"Stuff," Jake said vaguely. "What did Luffmiller have to say for himself?"

Julie sighed and picked up the paper on which she'd scribbled notes. "He didn't say much, but he took a lot of words to say it. There seem to be a lot of George O'Keefes and G. O'Keefes in Texas. Dozens of them."

"It figures," Jake said. "It's the third most populous state. O'Keefe's not an unusual name."

"Some of them have criminal records, but none has checked out so far. According to the the National Crime Computer, the rest of the country is positively teeming with O'Keefes. From coast to coast. Oh, why couldn't Rebecca have taken up with somebody named Xavier Zibbelwitz?"

"Cheer up. It could have been a Smith."

Her eyebrows drew together in a worried frown. "Jake, he says the FBI's going to be in touch with him. That must mean they suspect a serious crime."

Jake gave a short, satiric laugh. "The FBI? In his dreams. I told you, sugar, he's trying to impress you."

She looked at the notes and shook her head. "He told me about all these O'Keefes, at least."

"I could have told you about all those O'Keefes," he said with disdain. "That's the first thing you'd expect him to do."

"But the state police must be keeping him informed. They told him this much."

Jake laughed again. "They haven't told him squat, and they won't. One of the ugly truths about police work is jealousy among jurisdictions. The state police aren't going to share everything they know with some backwoods sheriff. No way."

"He asked me to have dinner with him," Julie said. "He said he could tell me a few 'secret aspects' of the case, and he was sure he'd have some new information as well."

"His news will be there's no significant news, and if he knows any secret aspects, he's getting them off his Batman plastic decoder ring. Come on. Let's grab some lunch and go talk to Mary Horner. I bet she knows more about this town than the sheriff ever will."

He came to her, bent and kissed her lips. For a dizzying moment, all of last night's excitement and yearning came back to her.

When he drew away, he gave her a smoldering look. "To be continued," he said.

And she knew that she would be in his arms again tonight, making love as if there were no tomorrow.

But she knew, just as well, that tomorrows always came. *"What then?"* her mind coolly asked. *"What then?"* her heart echoed, confounded and bewildered.

THEY ATE LUNCH at the town's one fast-food place, a franchised hamburger emporium that looked exactly like every one of its clones across America, and whose food tasted just as dull and mass-produced.

Heads turned when they walked in. Jake was sure people knew who they were, what they were doing, and were speculating about what was going on between them.

He supposed most of the town knew by now that he and she were staying in neighboring rooms at the Black Gold Motel. He supposed that friends of the chambermaid had been told he'd slept with Julie. Donnie Luffmiller, dense as he was, probably deduced it, but was hoping he might use his position to get lucky with Julie himself. The jug-eared son of a bitch.

It was two o'clock sharp when Jake and Julie walked into the bar again. The only other customers were two old men in striped overalls who sat nursing beers and glumly watching a soap opera on television.

Mary Horner brightened when she saw Jake, gestured for him to take a booth and began to fill beer mugs. She came to their booth carrying a tray with three beers. "These suds are on the house. I thought I'd take a break with you," she said.

She put down the beers with hardly a glance at Julie and sat next to Jake. "Cheers," she said and clicked her mug against his.

"Cheers," Jake said with his most disarming smile. Julie, ignored again, sat with her mouth in a very straight line. He imagined a small thundercloud playing over her smooth forehead.

"Last night, you got me started goin' down memory lane," Mary said. "I couldn't sleep, so I got up and started going through old photo albums and stuff. It all came back so clear, I almost feel young again. You better watch out."

She dug an elbow into his arm and gave him a friendly leer. Jake kept smiling.

Mary cocked her head and stared up at the corner of the smoke-stained ceiling. "I kept thinking about Annie and Rebecca. How silly they were back then. I was chasing real boys, smoking cigarettes and raising hell. I matured fast, you might say. Had a thirty-five inch bust when I was eleven years old. You can bet the boys noticed *that!*"

"I'm sure they did," Jake said, giving her bust a polite glance. Over the years its size had increased to huge and sagging.

Mary reached into her pocket, pulled out a pack of cigarettes and lit one. "I was old for my age and full of it. At that stage, I hated it when my mom sent me over to stay with Annie. Annie and Rebecca were older, but they seemed like retards to me. The summer I was fourteen, they were sixteen—never been kissed and proud of it. Like they were too good for the boys in this town. Truth is, none of the boys knew they were alive. Annie was skinny as a greyhound, and Rebecca was a butterball."

"So you had the real boys," Jake urged. "But Rebecca and Annie just had their movie-star dreams."

"Now, what I remember from that summer, is Rebecca was in love with Elvis Presley." Mary gave a laugh that resembled the caw of a crow. "Rebecca and Elvis! Can you imagine that?

"Annie was in love with the whole Kingston Trio, but mostly she was in love with the best-looking one. Not the tall one, not the short one, but the good-looking one. They sang a lot of these Caribbean songs. So Rebecca was going to marry Elvis and live in Hawaii, and Annie was going to marry the Kingston Trio and live in the Caribbean. Then they would take turns visiting each other. That was their plan."

Jake nodded. "Teenage dreams."

"Exactly." Mary chuckled. "My point is, they were kind of old for that sort of stuff. But they kept it up clear until they left for college. Rebecca went off to school with all her Elvis Presley albums, and Annie took her Kingston Trio albums. Which was really out of it, because by that time, the Beatles were about to come along. But neither Annie or Rebecca ever had a clue about the Beatles."

"You mean they didn't change with the times?"

"You've got it," Mary said with a nod that made her chins bob. "It was like they got stuck in time. But what I remembered, after all this time, was that Rebecca had to hide her Elvis records at Annie's house. Her daddy would have pitched a fit if he'd found out. He'd have tanned her hide."

Jake's instincts gave a silent jump. He allowed his eyes briefly to meet Julie's. Then he turned back to Mary. "Rebecca's father tanned her hide often? He beat her?"

"Oh, he didn't *beat* her," Mary said, waving her cigarette in a dismissive gesture. "But he'd whup her if she misbehaved. Which wasn't often. Rebecca didn't have what it took to rebel. She was a good girl. To a fault. Except for those damn Elvis records."

"What about Annie's parents?" he asked. "Did they know Annie was hiding these records for Rebecca?"

"Sure, they knew," Mary said with a shrug. "But they felt sorry for Rebecca. Her father was such a strict old bastard. 'Duty, duty, duty,' that's what he hammered into Rebecca. 'Respect your elders. Honor your father and mother.'"

Jake watched her take a mouthful of beer. It left a mustache of foam on her upper lip, which she wiped off with the back of one plump hand.

He said, "So your aunt and uncle didn't care for Will Albert?"

"Nobody cared for him," Mary said. "The older he got, the more self-righteous he got. Looked down his nose at the whole world. Oh, people liked Rebecca's mama well enough, but she was under the old man's thumb. Her and Rebecca both. My aunt said once that he meant to keep Rebecca chained to him her whole life long, and she was right. That's exactly what he did. Me, I'd have spit in his eye and walked off."

"I bet you would," Jake said, raising an eyebrow in approval. "So what happened to Annie and Rebecca in college? Annie got married, when?"

"Oh, sometime in the middle," Mary said carelessly. "She didn't finish college. Her folks were disappointed, but then I kinda lost track of things. I married my first husband, see, and bam! There I am, barely eighteen years old, a baby on the way, living in a strange city 'cause he's got a job at the big *oil refinery.*"

Mary's wide face twisted in disgust. "And him wanting to practice boxing on me every payday when he got drunk. I'd no sooner have the baby than I'd get pregnant again. I didn't keep up with Miss Annie Priss-Priss and Rebecca. I had troubles of my own."

"Sounds like it," Jake said. "You're a real survivor, Mary. Did you and Annie keep in touch?"

Mary shrugged. "Not for years. You know how it is. You go different ways. She married a guy in the oil business, went overseas, Malaysia or someplace like that. He died, and she married another guy and moved to New Zealand. She never had no kids or nothing. When we both got older, maybe we got sentimental. We started sending Christmas cards the last five years or so. That's about it."

"And she died suddenly? She was still a young woman."

Mary grunted. "Annie? She had leukemia. Her second husband died about two and a half years ago—I don't know why she couldn't pick a healthy one. She wrote about coming home to visit, but then *she* got sick, and never made it. Me, thank God, I'm healthy as a horse."

Jake gave her fat shoulder an appreciative pat. "That's because you stay young at heart, Mary. But what about Rebecca?"

"Well, she sure didn't stay young at heart because she never *was* young at heart, if you ask me. Not really."

"I mean did Rebecca stay in touch with Annie?"

Mary screwed her face up, shrugged. "I guess. After I moved back here, I'd see her on the street, and she'd always say, 'I heard from Annie.' And then I'd have to stand there and listen to the news, which was never much, in my opinion. Frankly, Rebecca was the sort of woman who could put me to sleep in about five minutes."

Across the table, Julie stiffened, and Jake knew she was deeply offended. Mary tossed Julie a bored look, as if she had just noticed her, but was not interested. "No offense," she said and took another mouthful of beer.

"I imagine," Jake said carefully, "that Rebecca was upset when she heard Annie was ill."

"Upset is hardly the word for it. She couldn't even talk about it," Mary said. "Not that I minded. Some women find the details of sickness real fascinating. I ain't one of 'em."

"Did she say anything to you when Annie died? Anything at all?"

"Not that I recall," Mary said. "My husband was in the hospital in Lubbock with his gallbladder when it happened. I had troubles of my own. Rebecca sent a note. Something all poetical, you know the way she was. I didn't keep it."

She dug into the pocket of her apron. "I did bring something to show you, though. Pictures. Snapshots and stuff."

She drew out a pack of photos thick as half a deck of cards. She fanned the pictures out on the table as if she were going to read fortunes with them. She pointed as she spoke, "I took that one the summer Annie and Rebecca were sixteen. See the pictures of Elvis and the Kingston Trio on the wall? This is them when they were eighteen. See how skinny Annie was? Rebecca always looked like a balloon beside her. Here's one with me in it. Will you look at the shape I had then?"

She droned on, but Jake listened and looked, every nerve ending alert. Finally, she came to a wallet-size studio photo of a woman with curly fair hair and glasses. "That's Annie, about three years before she died. She's the image of her mother in that picture. The image."

"Mary," Jake said, "it'd be a great favor if you'd let me borrow a few of these. I'll take good care of them."

"Sure," she said. "But be sure to return them in person. It's not often I get to talk to a good-looking devil like you." She elbowed him in the arm again and gave him a sly, flirtatious look.

"It'll be my pleasure," Jake assured her. "You're a pretty good-looking woman yourself. You've been more help than I can tell you. Thanks. And thanks for the beer. It hit the spot."

She looked pleased. "Want another?"

"We've got to be on our way. But I'll be back."

Reluctantly, she rose. Jake got to his feet and offered his hand to Julie. She took it with a possessiveness that made him want to smile. Mary Horner looked her up and down as if to say, *Once I was shaped better than you, kid.*

Jake leaned over and kissed Mary's leathery cheek. "You've been a doll," he said. "And I'll be back soon with your pictures. Keep the beer cold for me."

Mary's face split into a triumphant grin. "You got it. It's a date."

As he ushered Julie out the door, Mary called, as if it was an afterthought, "Hey! I hope you find Rebecca."

"I'll do my best, Mary. And thanks again. See you."

"Oh, really," Julie muttered angrily as she stamped toward the car. "What a horrible woman. Who knows what's happened to Rebecca? But there she sat, gloating like the cat that ate the canary. She doesn't care about Rebecca a bit. She was *flirting* with you. Ugh."

"It's your imagination," Jake said. "She's almost old enough to be my mother."

"It's not my imagination," she said, giving him a stern look. "And you were flirting back. You're shameless."

He gave her a slow, teasing smile. "Of course I'm shameless. Are you just figuring that out?"

"No, I'm just relearning it for the millionth time," she said. She stopped by the car and looked up at him, her cheeks pink with indignation. "Well? Now where? Who do we talk to next?"

He felt his smile fade. "I think," he said, "it's time you took me home to meet your mother."

Julie's brown eyes widened in shock. "My mother? You can't mean it."

"I do mean it. Do you want to drive or shall I?"

"My parents live just outside Fredricksberg—that's almost clear back to Austin. Why do you want to talk to my mother? You've got that secretive look on your face again. Tell me what's going on."

He knew she hated it when he held out on her, but he had no choice. He couldn't tell her anything, not until he was sure of a few more facts himself.

He wanted to talk to Lynn FitzJames. It wasn't a matter of idle curiosity. It was a matter of life and death.

JULIE LET JAKE DRIVE the first half of the trip. She sank back against the seat and watched him. He was a good driver, fearless, precise and with hair-trigger reflexes. He was the only person she knew who drove with more confidence than she did.

Of the two of them, she was the showboater driver, flirting more wildly with the speed limit, cranking rock music up to the max and losing herself in the sensations. Jake drove more easily, looking deceptively lazy at the wheel. He played country and western music, low and mellow, and although his dark eyes were alert, he always seemed to be thinking of something else.

"I don't know that I want to see my mother just now. She and I aren't on the best of terms these days," she told him. "I think she should be more upset about Rebecca."

"Your mother and you were never on the best of terms, as I recall. 'A study in opposites,' that's how you described it once."

Julie shrugged. She wasn't like her mother, and she didn't want to be. Lynn was cool, distant, and she liked keeping all her emotions hidden under aloof politeness. Piano had once been her great passion. Now music was demoted to a hobby, and golf and bridge parties were Lynn's ruling stars.

"I'd like to know what you want to ask her," Julie said, eyeing Jake suspiciously.

"I'll play it by ear," he said. "And I don't know how she'll answer. Or if she'll answer."

His profile was as impassive as that of a Roman emperor on a coin. Julie knew she was about to repeat history and enter a pointless argument, but she couldn't help herself.

"You've got a new hunch about Rebecca's disappearance. Something happened in Mrs. Cummings's office, but you're not talking."

"Nothing happened in her office," he said, keeping his eyes on the road.

Liar, she thought. "You found something at Rebecca's, but you're not talking about that, either. That's not fair. She's my aunt. I hired you, dammit. You have no right to keep secrets."

"I haven't got secrets. I've got a couple of ideas that are still toddling around in their baby clothes. That's all."

"And," Julie accused, "you were snuggling up to that— that harpy, Mary Horner, like she was Cleopatra. What did she say that made you so interested? That Rebecca liked Elvis? So did eleven billion other women. And why did you borrow those pictures?"

He gave her a cool glance, his black eyes as hard as onyx. "Look, I'm working on a theory. I don't want to discuss it. I don't want to scare you, and I don't want to give you false hope."

She tossed her hair. "I'm always scared and full of hopes that are probably false. I have been for weeks. Whatever you say can't be worse than all the uncertainty. I've been living with it too long."

"Live with it a little longer," he said dispassionately, his gaze trained on the road. He began to hum under his breath, as if he was listening to the music, not to her.

"Jake!" she said, glaring at him.

He slipped her another of his maddeningly cool looks, but the line of his mouth was obdurate. "I can give a slick, evasive answer—the kind you always hate. Or I can give you no answer until I know more. Which way do you want to play it, Julie? You call it. You want to keep asking questions?"

Oh, damn, she thought. *It's just the way it used to be.*

"Why are you so bloody stubborn?" she asked, giving him her frostiest look.

"Why are you?" he asked, giving her his, which was much more daunting.

She crossed her arms militantly and stared straight ahead at the long, empty highway.

"You want me to tell you something?" he asked, his voice edged. "I will. I'm a good cop. But there's another kind— the kind of cop I hate. I think of him as Mr. Important-Ass. There's a family with somebody missing or dead, and they're like drowning people. They'll cling to straws. And that's what Mr. Important-Ass does. He throws them straw after straw."

"I didn't mean—"

He cut her off. "You want me to talk? I'm talking. The guy's always got a fresh lead, a new hunch, a promising tip. He cranks up their hopes, then when they crash, he cranks them up again. Or he fills them with needless anxiety—not all his theories are happy ones. He keeps them in a state of constant turmoil. He acts like he's giving them confidences, but you know why he does all this? To make his ass feel important. I've got no patience with that. None."

Julie's cheeks flamed, half in anger, half in guilt. "Well, you *said* you had a new idea—"

"No," he corrected. "You said it. Remember? You know me 'so well.' You know 'that look' of mine. You know something's on my mind?—what is it? 'Spill, Jake. Tell. Talk.'"

He swore, and with a sinking heart, she realized the truth of what he said. "All right," she admitted. "I'm sorry. But I'm nervous and impatient. Let me drive the rest of the way, all right? Maybe my mind will stop spinning around like a hamster on an exercise wheel."

"I'll pull over at the next rest stop. Until then, I've got a question for you."

Suddenly, he sounded so laid-back, so casual, she was suspicious again. "What? What question?"

"Do you still want to sleep with me tonight? This afternoon, the look in your eyes said you did. Have you changed your mind?"

She ran her hand over her forehead. She stole another glance at him. He might have just asked her for the time or if she had the road map handy.

She opened her mouth to say, No, everything had changed. She would be staying with her parents; he could get a motel. She'd pay, of course.

But her mother and father were in their retirement condo on the golf course now. For all she knew, they already had their guest room booked for some golf partner flying in from Austin or Dallas. And Lynn always liked plenty of warning before overnight guests came, even her children. Perhaps *especially* her children.

In Julie's heart, which did she want? Lynn's perpetual coolness? Or Jake's passion, which she could have for such a short time longer?

He always said he admired her honesty, so she said, "I want to sleep with you. We'll check in to a motel before we call them."

And she added, because it was also the truth, "At least we don't fight when we make love."

He gave her a rueful glance, the ghost of his teasing smile. "You mean we don't fight *much*," he said.

Then he reached over and took her hand, lacing his fingers through hers.

She felt oddly content at this companionable, innocent touching. Almost at peace.

But deep down, she told herself sadly, *It can't last. It never does.*

11

JULIE WAS RIGHT, Jake thought. Her mother, Lynn Fitz-James, was beautiful, and she did look as if she could have once been a contender in Hollywood.

Her blond hair, severely swept back into some sort of twist, reminded Jake of a ballerina's, and when she moved, it was with a ballerina's grace. She wore a pale blue pant-suit that was so simple and striking, it must have cost a tidy bundle.

She had diamond studs in her ears, several diamond rings, and a gold chain around her neck from which hung a pendant shaped like a gold octopus with diamond eyes. She was smaller than Julie and built more boyishly, like a model.

When she spoke, she had a high, childish voice, small and piping, and Jake understood why she had never pursued an acting career. But her demeanor was anything but childish; she had a sharp, cold air about her that was in marked contrast to Julie's openness and quicksilver emotions.

"Come in," she said, with no other greeting. She gave Julie a quick, perfunctory hug and an air kiss.

"I'm Mrs. FitzJames. You must be Mr. Good Thunder," she said, eyeing Jake as if sizing up an enemy.

She turned to a man standing in the background. He was tall, with glasses and graying hair. "This is my husband, Clark."

Clark FitzJames came forward, gave Julie an awkward bear hug and said, "Hello, Punkin." She gave him a smacking kiss on the cheek, which actually made him blush.

He turned and gave Jake a firm handshake. "Pleased to make your acquaintance."

He looked Jake up and down. In the man's mild eyes, Jake saw a dozen unasked questions. *You're the one my daughter lived with? Was going to marry? She loved you? Why? What did you do to make her leave you? Why did she turn to you again? How are you treating her? What are your intentions? Do you think you're good enough for her? You still love her, don't you? You're probably sleeping with her again, aren't you? Are you going to hurt her again?*

"Clark, why don't you go back to your stamp albums? I'll handle this," Lynn FitzJames said. She did not so much as glance at her husband. Clark FitzJames gave Jake another mild look that asked all the same questions, then left, as obediently as a well-trained dog.

"Come into the living room," Lynn said, making a stiff gesture of invitation. She turned and marched, leading the way. Julie looked at Jake and gave him a wry look that said, *I told you so.*

Lynn FitzJames's living room, with its high ceiling and chandelier, was like her, a little too perfect for comfort. The sofa and chairs, upholstered in palest blue, looked as if they had never been sat in. The carpeting was glacial white; Jake could imagine no grandchildren ever playing on its pristine sweep.

Indeed, there were no grandchildren, Julie had said. Neither of her brothers had elected to have children. They and their wives, she'd said, preferred to stay unencumbered.

"Sit." Lynn made it sound like an order. She took the larger armchair and settled in it as if it were a throne. Julie sat on the sofa, and Jake sat beside her.

Lynn's face was neither happy nor friendly. "I must say, Julie, I wish you'd given us more warning. I'm always glad to see you, of course. But you know how I hate surprises."

She turned to Jake and gave him a frosty substitute for a smile. "I told Julie on the phone that the guest room's being repainted. The air's not fit to breathe. *And* the carpet's ripped up. I can't offer you hospitality. I'm sorry."

Jake nodded. She was telling the truth. He could smell the strong scent of paint drifting from upstairs. "I understand, ma'am."

He had the odd certainty that the woman *would* have offered him the room if it had been available; it would be uncivil for her to do anything else. And he was just as certain she would have let him and Julie share it without blinking an eye.

"We're staying at the motel just outside Windemere," Julie said.

"Well, don't eat at the restaurant there," Lynn said. "The food is poisonous. You may come here for breakfast. I'm sure I can rustle up something."

"No, I wouldn't put you to the trouble," Julie said. "Another time."

"Certainly," Lynn said, her smile less chilly. "Give me advance notice. So I can do things right. Would either of you like a drink? I have only beer or wine, but I do have a nice Chardonnay chilling. Or would you prefer coffee?"

"Nothing, Lynn," Julie said. "Thanks, anyway. I told you—we just want to talk. Jake wants to ask you some questions about Rebecca."

Lynn's face went blank. "I've already told the police all I know, which is nothing. I really wish you wouldn't persist in this, Julie. I try not to interfere with your life, but in this case—no good can come of it."

An odd way to put it, Jake thought. He said, "Mrs. FitzJames, I wish you'd tell me, in all frankness, what you think may have happened to your sister."

She gave him a look that was totally unreadable. It certainly wasn't for lack of skill that she hadn't pursued an acting career. She would have made one hell of an undercover cop. Cool as an ice cap.

"I'm afraid I really don't know. But I fear the worst. My sister was an extremely naive woman. Someone could have taken advantage of her very easily. She was seen with a man that night. I think he must have enticed her away with him somehow. After that, I don't want to think about what might have happened."

Discreetly he studied her. She was still damned attractive, even beautiful, for a woman of sixty-four. Few lines etched her face, the flesh at her jaw sagged only slightly and the perfect gold of her hair was professionally assisted. She was a miracle of maintenance.

But was there something *missing* in Lynn FitzJames? If thinking of what happened to Rebecca was unpleasant, did she simply not think of it? Was that why time had taken so little toll on her?

He said as gently as he could, "But you and your sister weren't close, were you? These last few years you weren't privy to her thoughts, her feelings?"

Lynn gave him a scornful little smile. "My sister and I never had much in common to begin with. Her world consisted of her school, her church and her father."

"You and she," he said, "were at odds after her father's death?"

"It was about the house. I suppose Julie told you. Julie always tells everything she knows." She made a gesture of resignation that was almost comic. "She's emotional. Like my mother was."

Julie shrugged and gave a crooked little smile of embarrassment. Jake thought, *Is that it, Julie? Did you get your sweetness and fire from your grandmother? Did it skip a generation?*

"Mrs. FitzJames, I don't mean to be out of line. I wouldn't ask these questions if they weren't important. But why did you quarrel about the house? It's a small house, and property values are down in Casino. Your earrings are probably worth as much as that house."

Lynn straightened in her chair, looking more regal than ever. "I hope," she said, looking him in the eye, "that you don't think I'm a greedy woman. My father built that house with his own hands. It contains his spirit, his skill, his creativity. I was born and raised in that house."

"Excuse me, ma'am, but so was Rebecca."

"Yes," Lynn retorted, "and I have no problem that it be half hers. But only half. My father, a creative, generous man, built it. *Her* father only lived in it—like a parasite. He just moved in and took over."

"I take it you have no fond memories of your stepfather?"

Lynn crossed her legs daintily at the ankles. "First, I never considered him my stepfather. My mother was emotionally distraught when she married him. She had to live with that. But I in no way considered him a father. My mother should have divorced him, and she might have if it hadn't been for Rebecca. Will Albert ruined my mother's life, he tried to ruin mine, and Rebecca let him ruin hers. It never occurred to me until he died that he'd even cheat me out of my own share of the house."

Jake nodded noncommittally, but he suddenly understood Lynn FitzJames much better. She was angry and rebellious in her own way, and had been ever since her mother married Albert. Beside him, Julie sat, her hands clenched tightly in her lap. He wondered how much of the past Lynn had told her daughter—and how much she had kept hidden.

Quietly he said, "How did he try to ruin your life, ma'am?"

Her nostrils flared. "Whenever he was angry with me, he wouldn't let me play the piano. He'd lock it and hide the key. He didn't want me to go to college—he said it would make me more 'uppity' than I was. That was the one thing my mother fought him on and won. She did it for Rebecca, too. But by then he'd worn her out. I never really believed she died of cancer. I think she died of *him*."

Jake took a deep breath and offered up a prayer. What he was about to say might make Lynn FitzJames order him out of the house. He said it anyway. "You're an extremely attractive woman, Mrs. FitzJames. Did your stepfather ever try anything improper with you?"

Beside him Julie tensed and sucked in her breath. Lynn FitzJames stared at him, her face absolutely blank, but she blushed to the roots of her hair.

Julie stared, first at him, then at her mother.

"He tried," Lynn admitted. "Oh, it was only little pats on the bottom now and then, brushing into me from time to time, so he could feel my breasts. But he never got any further. I never *let* him. He knew I'd kill him if he did."

"Mama," Julie said in a small, horrified voice.

Lynn ignored her. "It's a question of who controls whom," she said grimly. "I vowed he'd never control *me*. And by God, he didn't."

"Did you ever tell your mother?" Jake asked.

Her gaze didn't waver from his. "I tried. She told me I had to be mistaken. If I'd raised a fuss, he would have claimed it was my fault, I was lying and scheming against him. He was that sort."

"Did you ever warn Rebecca?" he asked.

"Yes," she said, her head high. "More than once."

Julie took his hand and held it tightly. Hers was cold as death.

"And?" he prompted.

Lynn tossed her head, an impatient gesture he'd often seen Julie use. "And she *claimed* it was different. That it had happened because I wasn't his own daughter. And because I was—'so pretty he probably couldn't help it.' That's actually what she said."

"Did you believe her?"

"I wanted to. About the time Rebecca turned twelve, he began having prostate problems, serious ones. My mother told me. I think he may have become impotent. I hope he did, the old devil. I hope it hurt him even to think about sex."

"Did he ever try anything with you again? After you were grown?"

"Once when I went home to visit my mother and Rebecca—Clark, Jr., was only a baby then. He cornered me in the kitchen and accused me of being a 'temptress.' He said I dressed the way I did and painted my face to make men think sinful thoughts. He'd gone into his holier-than-thou phase then."

"Did he try to touch you?"

"No. And if he had, I would have slapped his face. And later, when I took Julie with me to visit, I never left him alone with her, I can tell you that."

"I reckoned that, ma'am," he said. He couldn't help it, he smiled at her. She didn't smile back.

"Do I think he ever did 'anything improper' with Rebecca?" she said. "No. I hope she was right. I hope with his own daughter, he *was* different. But he still ruined her life. He ruined her one chance for happiness, and he used guilt to turn her into his private slave. I was furious with her for letting him do that. I loved her. But I wanted her to stand up for herself."

Jake studied her. She still looked queenly, but her left eyelid was twitching slightly, and she gripped the arms of her chair so tightly that her manicured nails were a bloodless white.

He and she exchanged a long glance, and he wondered, *How honest will you be with me, Lynn? How much can you dare?*

He gripped Julie's hand more protectively and stole a look at her. Her gaze, dismayed and pained, was fastened on her mother. He turned his attention back to Lynn.

"You've said twice he ruined Rebecca's life. What was her one chance for happiness? How did he work on her guilt?"

Lynn took a deep breath. "When Rebecca was twenty-two, her senior year in college, she had a lover. He was two years younger than she was. Once, she thought she was pregnant. She wanted to marry him."

"Rebecca?" Julie said, her voice disbelieving.

Lynn nodded. "My mother was ill at the time. Like a fool, Rebecca came home and told her father she had to get married. He accused her of trying to kill her mother, and he forbade her to get married. He said he'd shoot the boy. That she had to go off and give the baby away."

"Mama!" Julie said, obviously shocked. "You never told me this."

"It was Rebecca's secret," Lynn said imperiously. "She didn't want it told. Why am I telling you now? Maybe it's because of Mr. Good Thunder here."

Jake lowered one eyebrow in a puzzled frown. "Me, Mrs. FitzJames?"

Lynn cocked her head and looked pointedly at Jake's and Julie's linked hands. Then she met his gaze again. "Rebecca fell in love with a young Native American man. Will Albert couldn't stomach the thought. He thought Rebecca had dishonored him as much as if she'd turned into a—a woman of ill repute. No Native blood in his family, thank you."

Jake's own expression hardened. "The baby?"

"A false alarm," Lynn said and flicked an imaginary dust speck from the arm of her chair. "Brought on by nerves, I suppose. Or guilt. I don't know why she ever told Will. Why didn't she just go off and marry the boy? Did she think Will would accept him, just like that? Was she mad?"

"Who was the boy, Miss FitzJames? What happened to him? Did Rebecca ever see him again?"

Lynn's expression grew bitter. "His name was Alex, that's all I know. Will went to Odessa and threatened him, told him if he ever saw Rebecca again, he'd kill them both. Alex never went back to school. He joined the army, went to Vietnam. He never came back."

Julie squeezed Jake's hand harder still. In a choked voice, she said, "Dead?"

"Killed in action," Lynn said. "Did you ever wonder why Rebecca favored the little Mexican and Native American children? She never said, but I think they reminded her of the ones she might have had. She said he was handsome, this Alex. I don't know. I never saw him. But that's what she said—tall and handsome."

"My God, Mama," Julie said. "Didn't she hate Will after that? How could she go home and live with him?"

Lynn's mouth took on a contemptuous twist. "All her life he'd drilled into her that she *owed* everything to him. She was upset—Mama was dying. She was guilty—over Alex, over the baby, over the way Will made her feel. She let him manipulate her like a puppet. Until the day he died."

"I never would have spoken to him again," Julie said with passion. "I would have run off and married Alex, baby or no baby."

"I know you would have," Lynn said dryly. "That's how I raised you. To be your own woman. I saw what happened to my mother and to Rebecca. I vowed it would never happen to me or mine."

Jake said, "Mrs. FitzJames, I appreciate your honesty. I know it's been painful for you to say these things."

"Perhaps it's time they were said," Lynn replied coolly. She stared him straight in the eyes for a long, charged moment. Jake started getting strange subliminal messages from that gaze. It was as if she spoke volumes to him, without saying a word. *Lady,* he thought, *you are something else.*

Lynn said, "I know Julie thinks I've been callous toward Rebecca. Our relationship wasn't what it seemed. I wasn't unfeeling. I was hurt and angry that she wouldn't stand up for herself, seize control of her own life."

Julie had edged closer to Jake. He could feel the warmth of her body, the tension in it. Her thigh brushed his, then rested against it. He let it, and saw that Lynn FitzJames saw it all, watching with dispassionate eyes.

"Did only your family know of Rebecca's love affair? Of the false alarm about the pregnancy?"

"It was a jealously guarded secret," Lynn said. "Few people on campus even knew they were dating, let alone having a full-blown affair. Will convinced Rebecca that if people knew, they'd think she was a—a scarlet woman or something. Only the family knew. And Annie Prewitt."

Jake nodded. "Annie was married by then, wasn't she?"

"Yes," Lynn said. "She'd moved overseas with her husband. Annie was Rebecca's dearest friend. She was more like a sister to her than I ever was."

"And the two of them stayed in touch?"

"For years. They wrote almost every week. Rebecca used to give the foreign stamps to Clark for his collection."

"Did you know that Annie Prewitt died early this year?"

Lynn's perfect eyebrows rose. "Annie? No. I didn't. I'm sorry to hear it. She was always such a delicate little thing. But full of life. And imagination. She was good for Rebecca."

"Yes, ma'am," he said. "It sounds as if she was."

He stood, and still holding Julie's hand, drew her up beside him. "We'll let you get back to your business," he said. "I'm sorry to have troubled you. You've shed a great deal of light on Rebecca. I think we've been working on a very incomplete understanding of her."

Lynn, too, stood. "The world," she said, "has been working on an incomplete understanding of Rebecca."

Jake glanced down at Julie. "Do you want to say goodbye to your father?"

"He's asleep," Julie said, almost in chorus with her mother. The two women stopped, looked at each other and smiled as if at a private joke. In that moment, Jake realized they were family, all right. Just not your ordinary family.

Julie linked her arm through Jake's and said, "At this time of night, Daddy can work on his stamps fifteen minutes max before he nods off. I'll call him tomorrow and say goodbye."

Lynn walked them to the door. "Remember what I told you," she said. "Do *not* eat at that vile restaurant."

"I won't," Julie promised. She stopped by the front door and impulsively hugged her mother, then kissed her on the cheek.

"Julie," Lynn scolded. "My makeup!" But she hugged her daughter back, almost primly. She extricated herself from Julie's embrace and turned to Jake, extending her hand. "A pleasure to meet you, Mr. Good Thunder."

She had a firm but polite handshake. Again, she looked him square in the eye, and although her expression didn't reveal an iota of emotion, he felt as if she were saying things to him in silence.

She smiled slightly as she opened the door for them. "Next time, Julie, dear," she said, "give me ample warning before you descend, will you?"

"I'll try. Really, I will. Good night."

"Good night. Drive safely."

Then they were on the porch, in the chilly mist, and the door was shut. Julie clung to his arm. "Jake, I'm sick. Rebecca had someone she loved—and she lost him. She let that awful man drive him away. She must have spent the rest of her life regretting it. I think I'm going to cry again."

"No, you're not," he said fiercely. He took her by the shoulders. "The other night, you were getting down in the dumps because Rebecca never had a lover. Well, she had one. Be glad for that. You felt weepy because she was a virgin. Well, she wasn't. Be glad for that, too."

"But it's so sad," Julie protested.

"'It's better to have loved and lost than not to have loved at all,'" Jake quoted. "Believe me. I know that. By heart."

Then he bent and kissed her, long and passionately. He didn't know if he was doing it for Rebecca or for himself or a combination. It was getting all mixed up in his head.

IT WAS A LONG TRIP back to the motel, and Julie drove, hoping the simple, mechanical action would clear her mind. But when they reached their room, she still felt stunned.

She let Jake take her jacket and hang it up, and as soon as he was out of his own, she slipped her arms around him. She needed to hold him tightly and be held in return.

"I can't believe it," she said. "That nasty Albert man tried to molest my mother. If he wasn't dead, I'd kill him myself."

"I might help you do it, sugar. But don't worry about your mama. She can take care of herself."

Julie snuggled closer, letting her hands give her the comfort of stroking his hard, muscled back. "But what about Rebecca, Jake? Do you think Albert ever did anything to her? It's almost too horrible to think of."

"I think your mother's right. It was different with his own daughter. Rebecca stood for too much from him. I don't think she would have stood for that, too. She knew she could have gone to your mother for help. But she never did. No, I don't think Rebecca had to suffer that."

She drew back and stared into his dark eyes. "But you asked if Albert ever tried anything with my mother? Why? How did you know?"

He frowned, the set of his mouth unhappy. "I started to suspect something when you said all of Albert's pictures were gone from the piano. What would make Rebecca take them away? Why wouldn't she want to see his face? The first explanation that came to mind was the ugliest. And I thought, if he was that way with Rebecca, why not with your mother? She was an extremely beautiful girl."

Julie shook her head, unsure whether he was just trying to soothe her feelings by hiding the truth of what he believed.

He put his hand to her face, framing her jaw. "No," he said as if reading her thoughts. "I'm not trying to spare you. I believe Albert committed two sins against Rebecca. The first was conditioning her to be so dutiful, she hardly had a life of her own. The second was breaking up the only love affair she ever had. How could she have gone on, if he'd done still worse to her? She couldn't have borne it."

"You believe that?"

"I believe it. At first she felt ashamed over her affair with Alex. Albert used the guilt like a whip and a chair to keep her in place. But over the years, she saw society getting more and more permissive. People have affairs. Interracial marriages happen. Rebecca had to see that what she did wasn't some perversion, it was natural."

"But by the time she realized it, it was too late," Julie said sadly. "And her only act of rebellion was to take down her father's picture when he was gone."

"Maybe not," Jake said.

"Oh," she said miserably. "You mean George O'Keefe."

He brought his face closer to hers. "Julie, don't borrow trouble. You don't know that George O'Keefe did anything to her. There's no real proof. None. Don't grieve over an act that might never have taken place."

"I never really knew Rebecca," she said. "I never suspected she'd played queen of the jungle or had a crush on Elvis Presley or a love affair. That she had a lover and she'd lost him—almost thirty years ago."

"Will you remember me thirty years from now?" Jake asked. "When you've settled down with that nice, tame man you want so much?"

The question shook her. She put her hands on his biceps, gripped him as if she could draw some of his strength into her.

An odd image, touching yet absurd, came into her mind: her father nodding over his stamp albums, gently snoring. Was that the sort of man she wanted? Weren't women always accused of trying to find husbands who were duplicates of their fathers?

"I would remember you for a thousand years if I could," she said, her voice tight. "I would remember you forever."

"If you'd keep me," he said, "you wouldn't have to remember me. You could just turn your head and I'd be there."

"Oh, Jake," she said and laid her cheek against his chest. "It's just like the saying. I can't live with you, and I can't live without you. This afternoon, we argued just like old times, and now . . ."

"And now we're not arguing," he said. He slid his hand beneath her hair, cradling the back of her neck. "Make love, not war."

He brought his mouth to hers, and she drank in his kiss as if she were drinking a magic potion. His other hand slid down to her hips, guiding her pelvis nearer to his. Desire blazed in her like a throbbing spark between her thighs and spread.

Her eyes closed, her mouth still making love with his, she slipped her hands to his shirt and undid his top four buttons. She moved her hands beneath the fabric, gliding her fingers over his smooth, hard skin.

He pulled her hips closer still, moving his pelvis against hers, and she felt his arousal straining against his jeans. The spark in her began to fan to fire. She bent and kissed the skin over his breastbone and felt his heartbeat jolt beneath her lips.

He shuddered and took hold of her by the upper arms. "You always make me crazy when you do that," he said in a husky voice. "You make me want to eat you alive."

Then he crushed her to him, burying his face in her hair. "Let's get out of these clothes and into that crazy tub," he said. "We've never fooled around in one of those, have we?"

She gave a shaky laugh and whispered, "It may be a last frontier." She unbuttoned his shirt the rest of the way and kissed his breastbone again while her fingers traced the hard planes of his stomach and moved to his erection; she could feel its hardness and heat through the straining denim.

"Julie, stop," he whispered. "You'll get me so excited I'll set a speed record. Let me undress you. Let me touch you."

He turned her in his arms so she rested with her back against his chest. He kissed the back of her neck as he unbuttoned her blouse and slowly peeled it from her body.

He kissed the tender and deliciously tickly spot behind her ear as he unfastened her bra and drew it from her body. He dropped it, then covered both her breasts with his hands. He had such wonderful hands, warm and powerful. They could play over her with sureness and sensitivity, as if she were a stringed instrument, and he knew how to draw every sort of sensual harmony from her body.

As one hand sent her breasts into sensations of tingling rapture, his other moved beneath the waistband of her jeans, gliding down her stomach until his fingers touched the most exquisitely sensitive spot on her body and sent her into shivers of feminine longing.

His kisses at the nape of her neck and her ear drove her mad with excitement. His hand, caressing first one breast, then the other, made them swell and strain toward his touch. The expert sensation of his fingers in the moist, silky hotness between her thighs undid her.

But dimly, she was aware she was alone in this feverish yet blissful luxury; he was not joining her. An intense need to share welled up in her. She turned and wound her arms around his neck.

He was always so giving, so generous in sex. She kissed him, fully and deeply to thank him and tell him she needed to give him pleasure as rich and rare as he had given her. "I'll do anything you want," she whispered against his lips. "Anything. Tell me what to do."

He ran his hands over her bare arms, gripped her by the waist. "Take off the rest of your clothes." His whisper was hoarse with desire. "Let me watch you. Then undress me."

She stepped back, shaking her hair so that it fell down over her breasts in raven waves. She slipped out of her shoes. Slowly she undid her jeans, first the snap, then drew down the zipper inch by inch.

She eased the jeans down past her hips, let them sink to her ankles, then stepped out of them lightly. She stood before him, and raised her hands to her hair. Languorously, she pushed it aside so that it fell down her back and he could see her naked body.

Softly, she walked up to him. He never took his eyes from her. She pushed his shirt back off his broad shoulders, slid it down his arms until it fell free.

"Take off your boots," she said softly, putting her hands on the waistband of his jeans. He obeyed, kicking them aside. With torturous slowness, she undid his jeans. She pushed them down over his lean hips until he stepped free, and stood before her, as naked as she.

"Run the bath," he said, still not taking his hungry gaze from her. His mouth was taut with control.

She walked to the tub and toyed with the faucets. It began to fill, water pouring out in a pulsing crystalline rush. Jake walked to her side but didn't touch her. She understood. He was trying to pace himself, make himself go as slowly as possible so he could please her as much as possible.

When the water reached a certain level, the jets began creating glancing ripples. "Step in," he ordered.

She did, and sank to her knees. The water swirled around her like a live, silken thing. Then he was before her, on his knees, too, and he cupped his hands and poured water over her breasts.

They caressed each other with water until their bodies gleamed with it. Then he began to stroke her with the suds of perfumed soap. She did the same to him, until they could stand it no longer.

They said nothing, but they both knew the moment. She wound her legs around him, and he entered her, holding her by the waist. They coupled sensuously and perfectly, movement for movement, their bodies as wet and sleek as two mating creatures of the sea.

Her mind turned dark, as if she would faint from pleasure, and she arched into his touch, swept away by the primal rhythms of their lovemaking

Swirling stars danced before her closed eyes; helpless murmurs of pleasure fell from her lips, and her body rose and fell to his touch. A moment of ecstasy ravished her, took her out of herself, made her one with him and with the universe.

Afterward, fragrant with perfume and tingling with fulfillment, she lay beside him, content to be in his arms. "If only we could do this all our lives, and nothing else," she breathed wistfully.

He kissed her bare shoulder and said nothing.

"Jake?"

"Yes, sugar?"

"What are we going to do tomorrow?"

He didn't answer for a moment. His silence made her inexplicably nervous. "Jake?" she said, sensing something was about to happen.

"Tomorrow I've got to leave you," he said.

She turned and raised herself on one elbow, staring down into his shadowy face. "Leave me?" she said in dismay.

"I've got to go to Lubbock and check on that chiropractor. And some other things, as well. I'll move faster if I move alone. I'm sorry, but that's the way it is."

A terrible sense of emptiness overtook her. "But we're working together—"

"Not from here on out," he said. "I mean it. I can get to the bottom of this faster alone. You'll only slow me down."

"When will you be back?"

"I don't know. I'll call when I have something."

"Call me every night. Please."

"No."

No. The word sounded like a knell in her ears. "Why not?"

"Because we're getting in too deep, and in the end you're going to walk off and leave me again. Because maybe you're right. I can't change completely, Julie. I'm a cop, and I'll always be a cop. And if we go much further with this, and I lose you a second time, it'll kill me."

Tears stung her eyes. "If we go much further with this, and some—some thug shoots you, then I'll die, too. And I'll die a little every day, dreading it's going to happen."

"See, Jules," he said, touching her cheek. "We have to think. Promise me you will."

She felt half-sick with dread.

"Promise me," he said, running his hand over her hair, "that you'll think of tonight especially. The conversation with your mother, this, everything that happened, all of it. Will you?"

"Yes," she whispered. How could she not remember tonight?

"And promise me something else," he said, touching her face again.

"Yes?"

"If I can't find Rebecca—or I find her and something bad's happened to her, you won't hate me."

"Jake," she said, putting her hand on his shoulder, "I couldn't hate you."

"Remember that when the time comes," he said, then took her into his arms again.

They lay together in the darkness, not speaking, holding each other, both knowing it might be the last time.

12

SHE DROVE BACK to Austin, to the airport. Jake bought a ticket to Lubbock; the commuter flight was only half-filled and leaving almost immediately.

At the gate he swept her into his arms and kissed her goodbye. *We're making a scene,* Julie thought, clinging to him, wanting the feel of his hands running up and down her body. *We're making a scene and I don't care.*

Then a voice over the public address system announced the flight was boarding.

"There's something you're not telling me, Jake. Will you find what happened to Rebecca? Will you?"

"I don't know. I may draw nothing but blanks, Jules. I may come back to you with empty hands. I may fail you. I'm sorry, but it's true."

"You won't fail," she said, tightening her arms around his neck. She gave him a passionate, if crooked, kiss on the mouth.

"I can fail you," he said against her lips. "Don't count on me. Don't set yourself up for heartbreak."

"Jake—"

The crackling voice came through the loudspeakers again. "Boarding now, American Eagle Flight 414, departing for Lubbock and Amarillo, last call."

"Jules, you promised me you'd think of everything that happened last night, about your mother, too. You and she shouldn't be at odds. She's a stand-up lady in her way. And she's fiercely proud of you. I mean it."

Julie blinked up at him in surprise. "My mother? Proud of me? Hardly! Oh, Jake, come back soon. I'll think about you all the time."

"Do that," he said, his hands framing her face. "And think about why your mother told me the truth about Rebecca."

He kissed her for the last time, a burning, desperate kiss. And then he was gone.

She watched through the window as he strode across the tarmac, his suit bag over his shoulder. He carried his duffel bag in one hand and Rebecca's battered valise in the other.

Her vision blurred with tears as she watched him hand his luggage to the man loading the hold, then mount the silvery ladder and disappear into the plane's interior.

Angry at her own weakness, she blinked back tears. But she stood, watching the red-and-white plane until it taxied down the runway, lifted off, and soared into the clouds, vanishing.

Then she turned away, feeling empty and frustrated, and headed toward the parking garage. *My life is a wretched mess*, she thought.

How did other women do it? she wondered futilely. How did they marry men who courted death? How did they see them go off to work, knowing they might never return?

How did they have children, knowing that any day the father of those children might not come home? How did they live without conveying their terror and resentment to the children? *Be nice and mind Daddy. Somebody may shoot him tomorrow.*

SHE RETURNED to her little house and studio in the hill country. She worked, desultorily, on a series of watercolors of cactus flowers. True to her word, she thought of Jake constantly.

Her telephone rang infrequently, but when it did, she nearly jumped out of her skin, hoping it was Jake. But it never was. It was someone trying to sell her insurance, storm windows, aluminum siding or a magazine subscription.

It occurred to her that since breaking up with Jake two years ago, she'd drifted into a life-style even more solitary than Rebecca's had been.

She could go for days without seeing another human being. She lived alone and her house was sixty miles from Austin; it had been easy to let her friendships dwindle, to settle into a sort of permanent hibernation.

Her family had never been close. She talked to her parents once a week at most, her brothers every few months or so. They were quiet men, mild and uncommunicative like her father.

What a strange coincidence, she thought, that Rebecca had fallen in love with a Native American. How outdated it seemed that Will Albert would object to such a union.

It had never occurred to Julie to think of Jake as a person of another race. To her, he had simply been Jake, the man she thought she loved.

Sometimes they joked about it. He claimed that other branches of the Good Thunder family were named "Bad Thunder," "Indifferent Thunder" and "Fairly Decent Thunder." He'd had a bumper sticker on his car that said "Custer Died For Your Sins."

But race had never been an issue between them. Her parents hadn't so much as blinked an eye when she'd said she was engaged to a man named Good Thunder. Well, her father *had* blinked, actually, but she was sure her mother wouldn't react if Julie said she was marrying a man named Ogggg who came from Mars and had three heads.

"I raised you to live your own life," her mother had always said in her cool way.

Jake had asked her to think of the conversation with her mother, and she did, playing it over and over in her mind like a recording.

You and she shouldn't be at odds, he'd said. *She's a stand-up lady in her way.*

She brooded on this. In truth, she had misjudged her mother. Lynn had seen Rebecca's house not as a material possession but as a symbol of all that Will Albert had usurped and ruined.

Will Albert had figured far more centrally in Lynn's life than Julie had ever suspected. She could see now that much of Lynn's personality had been formed in rebellion against the man. Of the three women whose lives had touched Albert's—his wife, his daughter, his stepdaughter—only Lynn had had the strength to thwart him.

Lynn's everlasting coolness had surely been born when she lost her beloved father, then saw her mother fall under the spell of the hated Albert. The man's treatment of Lynn was wicked and perverse, unforgivable.

Lynn had escaped him, determined to live life on her own terms—and she must have vowed never to let herself be hurt again. She'd kept her emotions cool and distant to avoid more pain. In her mind, one either managed or knew the hated powerlessness of being managed.

She'd treated Rebecca as she had, not out of hardheartedness but a sort of angry despair: *Don't live your life through me—take it into your own hands. Rebel, Rebecca. Escape and be free.* But Rebecca never did.

Lynn's emotions about Rebecca were deep and complex, and she had purposely set out to raise Julie as differently from Rebecca as possible.

How tangled together all their lives were, Julie thought—through her mother, she had been profoundly influenced by people she'd never known—her grandmother and grandfather—and a man she'd scarcely known at all: Will Albert.

After two days of hard thinking and indifferent painting, Julie decided to phone her mother.

Lynn answered on the third ring. "Hello, FitzJames residence, Lynn speaking," she said in her precise way.

"It's Julie," Julie said. "I've been thinking about you."

"That won't pay the rent," Lynn replied.

"Thank you for talking to Jake and me the other night. I know it was an inconvenience, but I really appreciate it."

"You didn't give me much choice," said Lynn.

"Jake appreciated it, too. He's in Lubbock now. He's checking on something about Rebecca, but he won't say what or how long it'll take him."

"A good policeman should keep his own counsel," Lynn answered. "It's fitting."

"I owe you an apology," Julie said, plunging on. "I've always been critical of the way you treated Rebecca. I didn't understand your feelings about the house. I'm sorry."

"Thank you, but I don't need you to validate my emotions."

Julie sighed. Understanding her mother better didn't make it easier to talk to her.

"I *know* that," she said. "But because of our talk, I see many things more clearly now. I wish you'd told me the truth years ago."

"Why dwell in the past?" Lynn asked. "Besides, Rebecca didn't wish certain things discussed."

"I'm surprised you told it all to Jake. It wasn't like you. Why?"

Lynn was silent a moment. When she spoke, her high voice sounded slightly petulant, like an irritable child's. "Must I have a reason for everything I do? Sometimes one just *does* things. Please don't try to psychoanalyze me."

Julie persisted. "Jake says you're proud of me. I never thought that. Is it true?"

"Of course it's true."

"Well, why have you never told me?"

"You don't need to get a swelled head," said Lynn.

Frustrated, Julie gave up. Asking for emotion from Lynn was like asking for a bird to give milk. "Is Clark there? I'd like to say hello."

"He's gone to the liquor store. We're entertaining tonight. I'm making mushroom caps stuffed with nuts. I wish I'd chosen to hang by my thumbs instead."

"Then tell him hello and give him my love," Julie said. "And I love you, too."

"Thank you, dear. Likewise, of course."

"If Jake finds out anything about Rebecca, I'll phone you right away."

"Please do. But don't get your hopes up."

"If anybody can find her, he can," Julie said. "I believe that."

"That's nice, dear. Ye gods, there is a *fly* in this kitchen. I have to hang up."

There was an abrupt *click* in Julie's ear, and the line went dead. Shaking her head, she hung up the phone.

She felt drained of willpower, and she could not force herself to go back to her easel. Instead, she took a walk by the creek, as she often did when she became restless.

Thumbs hooked in the back pockets of her jeans, she strolled the familiar path, watching the sun glint on the thin trickle of water that flowed over the limestone rubble of the creek bed.

She stared up at the blue sky, thinking of Jake. She missed him so much her body ached with it. She remembered their last night together and wondered if it would be enough to last for the rest of her life.

Whether Rebecca was found or forever lost, he must go back to Tulsa. She could go with him, of course, but it would only end as before. She still had terrible nightmares of Billy Cable being murdered. Billy would dwell in her heart forever, she thought. The ghost of what was and what could befall Jake.

I can't wake up every morning wondering if I'll be a widow before the day is through, she thought, watching a hawk sail over the mesquite trees. *I can't bring children into the world knowing that their father could be ripped out of our lives in the space of a heartbeat.*

It would be easier to be like Lynn, to cut emotion out of her life as if it were something hazardous to peace and health.

She was her mother's daughter only in her independence. Once, in angry adolescence, she had accused her mother of neglecting her, of letting the maid, Sophie, raise her.

"Sophie's more suited to certain aspects of it," Lynn had answered, hardly ruffled. And Lynn, always analytical, had been right.

Sophie was a tall, round black woman, quick to laugh, easily touched to tears, fond of hugging. It was Sophie who'd taught Julie to bake cookies, make a bed, iron a blouse.

Sophie died when Julie was nineteen. Julie had come home from college for the funeral and hadn't been able to stanch the tears. That night she'd lain in bed and sobbed like a lost child.

Lynn had heard her, come into the room and put her hand on Julie's shoulder. "Get hold of yourself," she'd said. "You'll make yourself sick. Tears won't bring her back. Tears bring nothing back."

She'd bent and kissed Julie's tear-streaked cheek. It was one of the few times Julie could remember her mother giving a kiss that wasn't dictated by politeness.

As for her father—Julie picked up a pebble and hurled it into the creek with exasperation. She loved her father. He was a good, kind man, but he was no more talkative than a houseplant. He clearly adored his wife, but he was completely under her control and happy to be so.

Clark was dependable as the sunrise and just as predictable. Lynn could have been content with no other sort of man. He was tame and as faithful as a lapdog.

Tame, thought Julie with a pang. The very thing that Jake wasn't.

The hawk passed overhead, and his shadow glided on the grass before her. Just as swiftly and silently, a thought came into her mind—a strange, wonderful bolt of insight that stunned her with its simplicity.

She raised her face to the sky and smiled.

JAKE CALLED the next afternoon. "I'll be on the 8:27 flight from Lubbock. American Eagle, number twelve. Can you meet me at the airport?"

Julie's heart leaped against her rib cage so hard that it hurt. "Of course," she said. "Jake—about Rebecca—did you find anything?"

"I think so, sugar, but I don't want to try to explain it on the phone. It's complicated."

Her hand had started to tremble and she gripped the phone more tightly. "Jake? The news—is it good? Or bad?"

"Let's say it's not bad."

"Not bad?" Her pulse quickened and hope, so long dormant, soared in her, singing like a lark.

"Not bad," he repeated. "I'll tell you everything when I see you. And I'll see you soon. I've missed you."

"I've missed *you*," she returned. "Oh, Jake, when will you have to go back to Oklahoma?"

There was a beat of silence. "I should go tomorrow, sugar. I've used up my vacation time. I'm due back."

"Oh," she said. An abyss of emptiness opened within her.

"I'll see you in a few hours," he said.

"You're not going to give me any hint about Rebecca?" she said.

"I'll give you one. I talked to Martinez this morning. Remember? The detective in Austin. The man with the turquoise rings came forward. His name is Clay Listermann, he's a traveling salesman, and he's a former student of Rebecca's. He bumped into her in Austin and she invited him to have dinner. He's got a rock-solid alibi for the rest of the night. He's innocent, sugar."

"That's all you're going to tell me?" she said in dismay.

"All right. One more thing. We had a clue sitting in front of us we never saw. In the book of poems she gave you."

"The poems?" Julie asked, confounded. He'd asked to take Rebecca's book with him, but hadn't explained why he wanted it. What clue could possibly be hidden in it?

"I'll see you soon," he said. "Goodbye, beautiful."

When he hung up, she flew around the little house, cleaning up the clutter from her painting. She took a shower, brushed her hair, put on her jeans and her prettiest blouse, a fawn-colored silk one. Her cheeks were so pink, she didn't need rouge, and she brushed her hair until it shone like a raven's wing.

In Austin, when Jake stepped off the plane, she didn't think of what was safe or sensible, she threw herself into his arms so wildly he took a staggering step backward. He dropped his luggage and kissed her so passionately that someone gave a wolf whistle.

She barely heard it.

"What a welcome," Jake whispered against her lips. "I think you did miss me."

"It was like having my heart cut out," she said. "I bled loneliness all over the place."

"Come on," he said. "Let's go to the hotel where Rebecca stayed and have a drink. It seems like the right place to explain all this."

She held him more tightly, staring up into his dark eyes. "What did you find out, Jake?"

"Maybe just enough," he said.

THE SIGN at the entrance of the restaurant said, Seat Yourself. Holding Julie by the hand, Jake led her to a table.

The aloof young waiter, Kevin Waring, was on duty, but he slipped into the kitchen when he saw them enter the restaurant.

Julie watched the doors ease shut behind him. "He acts like he doesn't want to see us."

"He doesn't," Jake said. "But it's all right. He withheld information about Clay Listermann, but Listermann turned out to be unimportant. Rebecca ran into him and used him to her advantage. She was slick. Have a seat."

He pulled out a chair for her, but she could only stare at him in surprise. "Rebecca used him? *Slick?*"

"Sit," he said.

Obediently she sat. He seated himself across from her. A stocky waiter immediately appeared. "A Corona with lime for me," said Jake. "And a glass of Chardonnay for the lady."

"Yes, sir." The waiter bowed unctuously and then crept away as silently as a cat.

"Jake," Julie said, "Tell me what you mean. How did Rebecca use Clay Listermann?"

He gave her his crooked half smile and put his hand over hers. "She used him to create another false trail. Rebecca's fine, Julie. She's alive and well. But I doubt if you'll ever see her again."

She stared at him in utter shock, unable to speak.

He said, "Rebecca's near a small city called Avarua on an island named Rarotonga. It's the chief island of the Cook Islands. She's living there in a leased oceanfront house as Annie Prewitt Smith."

"*What?*" Julie said, stunned.

"I told you the police are blasé about missing adults because too often they're people who've wanted to disappear. That's what happened with Rebecca. She took off for the South Seas, just like she dreamed of, all those years ago."

She stared at him openmouthed. "Rebecca's in the South Seas? But how? It's impossible. She couldn't *do* such a thing."

"She could and she did," he said, lacing his fingers through hers. "She planned it for years. She and Annie Prewitt planned it together, I think."

"But—but," Julie stammered—"*how?*"

"Annie Prewitt knew she was dying," he explained. "She also knew Rebecca had been trapped for years in a town that was fading off the map. Annie had money. Annie had the lease on the house in Rarotonga—her husband had intended to retire there."

He squeezed her hand. "Annie loved Rebecca, Julie. She loved her like a sister. So she gave her the greatest gift she could—freedom. I think she mailed Rebecca all her identity papers, everything she'd need. Her money, too."

"Money?" Julie asked, echoing him.

"Rebecca had a separate bank account in Lubbock. It took some fast-talking, but I got them to open their records to me. Three months before Annie died, Rebecca deposited fifteen separate checks. They totaled just under a hundred and fifty thousand dollars."

Julie's heart slammed dully in her chest. She felt lightheaded, almost faint. The waiter set their drinks before them, but she hardly saw him. The whole room had turned phantomlike, unreal.

Jake said, "I don't think there ever was a George O'Keefe, sugar. For every withdrawal that Rebecca made in Casino, there was a deposit in Lubbock. She was transferring funds, that's all. The card? She planted it and signed it herself. Or maybe Annie did it for her."

"She *planned* all this—for over two years? I can't believe it."

"She told people she was going to Lubbock to see a chiropractor. There was no chiropractor. Instead, she was setting up a second identity under your grandmother's maiden name. A post office box so nobody in Casino knew she was hearing so often from Annie. A bank account. After Annie's death, she was up there every two weeks, making withdrawals. Always just under ten thousand dollars. Ten thousand dollars and the bank has to report it. Somehow, she learned all the angles, and she played them. Perfectly."

"My God," she breathed. "When did you start to suspect this?"

"My first inkling," he said, "was when you told me about the name George O'Keefe. She and Charity obviously weren't close friends, but she confided in Charity, sure she'd come forward when she heard Rebecca had disappeared. And it was almost too pat—a name Charity couldn't forget."

"But you never said . . ."

"Sugar, I couldn't be sure. But remember when you showed me the picture of Rebecca's Brownie troop, and I said they all looked alike in their uniforms? Rebecca and Annie did look a little alike. But as they got older, the striking difference was Annie was thin, Rebecca wasn't. But over the years, Annie changed. Look at the picture Mary Horner gave me."

He drew a thin stack of photos from his shirt pocket and lay one before her. Annie Prewitt, thin no longer, gazed at her serenely. Her face was as round as Rebecca's, her eyes, behind their glasses, the same shade of dark brown. Her hair, short and overcurled, was tinted blond.

"It seemed surprising Rebecca cut her hair. Now it's clear why. My guess is that she took the shuttle from this hotel the night she left, flew to Dallas, checked into another hotel room and dyed her hair blond. She put on a pair of bogus glasses, and when she left, she was no longer Rebecca Albert, with the distinctive limp. She was Annie Prewitt, who walked just fine."

Julie shook her head to clear it. "The limp? She faked the limp?"

"When I knew that," he said, "it all started to fall together. When I saw Annie's picture, I pretty well knew. And when I heard your mother's story, I knew how motivated Rebecca had to be."

She wrapped both her hands around his. "But Jake—how did you know she faked the limp?"

"Her rain boots. In the heel of the right one, she'd taped a marble. There's no way not to limp with a marble in your shoe. She probably started out with a BB or something and worked her way up."

He snapped open the valise and handed her the rain boot. She looked inside and saw the marble, held in place with a strip of adhesive tape.

Wordlessly, he handed her another shoe of Rebecca's, a sensible-looking loafer. "Look at the insole," he said. "You can see the tape marks."

She peered at the insole and saw that he was right. The rectangular mark of the adhesive was still visible. "My God, Jake," she breathed. She handed both shoes back to him. He dropped them into the valise and took out the book of poetry. He laid it on the white tablecloth.

He said, "What did Rebecca have to hold her here? She'd never been as close to your mother as she wanted. And your mother had criticized her for years for not taking control of her life. Her father was dead, he couldn't hold her back any longer. Her best friends at the school were gone. The school itself was dying, her job was in question. The only thing she had here to love was you, and you had a life of your own."

Tears welled into Julie's eyes, and for once she did not think to fight them. "Oh, Jake, if only I'd known how lonely it must have been for her—I should have spent more time with her. I hate myself."

"No," he said with feeling. "That only would have held her back. She's having her adventure at last. She's free. Be glad for her."

He spread the other photos before her. There were four of Rebecca and Annie at different ages in Annie's room, and two of them in what appeared to be a college dorm room. In all of them, they looked young, high-spirited and happy.

"Look at the walls behind them," he said. "Look at the bulletin boards."

She looked. Movie posters for *Blue Hawaii, South Pacific, Tahiti Holiday*. Album covers of the Kingston Trio and Elvis covered the walls. A page from a magazine that showed a palm tree against a sea lit by a gorgeous tropical sunset. Everywhere were reminders of their shared dreams.

"Two kids in the driest, dustiest part of Texas," Jake said, "with a mutual obsession. They even played jungle queen when they were little bitty things. The tropics were on their mind, big time."

"And Annie made it to New Zealand," Julie said sadly. "But Rebecca didn't."

"The Cook Islands are a protectorate of New Zealand," Jake said. "The language is English. I read about it. People say it's what Hawaii was like sixty years ago. A little bit of paradise, with azure blue water and flowers all year round. She finally made it, Julie. She's living the dream."

"Oh, Jake," she whispered. "You think it's true?"

"Yes," he said. "And what we found at Rebecca's house wasn't nearly as significant as what we didn't find. There were no letters or cards or snapshots from Annie. Your album was missing. I'm betting Annie's is, too. She took them with her. And there was no notebook of her poetry, no folders of it, anything. The three things she couldn't leave behind—the poems, and souvenirs of Annie and of you."

Julie was suddenly almost angry at Rebecca. "Didn't she know how I'd worry? My God, I've been driven nearly crazy."

"I think she knew, Julie. But there was no helping it. But she sent you a message. Look at the first poem in her book again. It doesn't say what we thought."

Julie read the verse again.

> To Julie, When I Am Gone
> When I am gone, dearest, to a better place,
> Do not grieve for me.
> Even on that further shore
> I will have tender thoughts—for thee.
>
> And though we meet no more in this little life,
> I pray to fates above
> That life always brings thee beauty
> And the courage, dear, to love . . .

Julie's vision swam with tears, she could no longer read the words. "She wasn't talking about death," she murmured in a broken voice. "She was talking about really going away."

"There're a lot of little children in Rarotonga, brown as Indians," Jake said. "I bet she's a volunteer at some school or day-care center. She's probably teaching a bunch of them 'The Itsy Bitsy Spider' right now."

Julie's tears spilled over and ran down her cheeks. One fell on the page, blurring the ink on the line that said, "I will have tender thoughts—for thee."

Jake took her hand again. "So don't begrudge her, Julie. Psychologists call it the Gauguin syndrome. After that painter who threw over his proper, suffocating life and headed for Tahiti."

She shook her head, almost unable to speak. She knew Gauguin's story well, his escape from unbearable dreariness to an island paradise. "But isn't what she's doing—well—illegal? Couldn't she get into trouble?"

"It's a little illegal," he said gently. "But who needs to know? Officially, it's not my case. I'll never tell."

The aloof young waiter scuttled out of the kitchen with a tray of food, set it down before another pair of diners, then sped back to the kitchen.

"As for him," Jake said, crooking one dark eyebrow, "he saw Clay Listermann later that night—without Rebecca. In a gay bar. Listermann was open about it. He was with a longtime lover he's had in Austin. He remembers seeing our friend there. But our friend isn't ready to come out of the closet. Well, as far as I'm concerned, his secret's safe, too."

She put her hands to her face to cover her tears. "You're wonderful, Jake."

"No," he said. "I'm a fool. I love you, Julie, and if you want, I'll quit undercover work. I'll quit the force altogether if it makes you happy. I'll do anything you want—if only you'll have me."

She shook her head, kept her face covered. "You asked me to think about that last night, and I did. I realized something about myself I didn't like."

She lowered her hands and tried to gain control of herself. "My mother's a very strong person. She raised me to be strong, too. But I never thought I was like her in any other way. Then I realized she passed something else on to me, without either of us realizing it. She only feels safe with a man she can control, Jake."

He gazed at her, his eyes solemn.

"After Will Albert, Lynn wasn't about to let any man be in charge. It seemed like a terrible thing to me, not to be in charge of everything in my life. I wanted to be in charge of you, too. But I can't be happy with a man like my father. I can't be happy with anyone but you."

He reached over and softly wiped the tears away with his thumb. "What are you telling me, Jules?"

"I'm telling you that you're like my other half, and when I left you, I lost half of myself. It was more than missing you physically. I missed you in every way—mind, heart, soul."

She paused and swallowed. "I could never stop you from being a policeman. It's what you are. It's *who* you are. But if you'd give up the undercover part, I'd be the happiest woman on earth."

"It could still be a dangerous job, Jules."

"I understand that."

He took a strand of her hair between his fingers and fondled it like silk. "I could give up the undercover part. I realized that in Austin. I didn't take you there with me because I was going to have to lie and bend the truth, and I figured I'd have to flirt like hell with at least one woman before it was over. I did, and I thought, Lord, no wonder Julie hates this. It's one more thing to hide from her. I hate it myself."

"You mean it?" she asked.

"Absolutely. I knew it had to come some day. A man can't stay undercover forever. Someday, somebody recognizes you. I've pushed my luck too long. Two years ago, I wasn't ready. And I sure wasn't going to let a woman tell me how to live my life. But, like you said, I missed you in every way, in mind and body and spirit. Life without you is hell, Jules."

She nodded and gave a little sniff. "It was hell without you, too. I climbed into a shell. I was getting to be like Rebecca. Living my life but not really living at all. Afraid of taking chances."

He pushed away from the table impatiently. "Julie, let's get out of here. Let's check into a room. I want to hold you in my arms. I want to make love to you."

He rose and so did she. She held Rebecca's book tightly to her chest with one hand, and she wound her other arm through his. He laid a few bills on the table and picked up the valise. Smiling his crooked smile, he walked her to the desk.

"Mr. and Mrs. Good Thunder," he said to the clerk. "Of Tulsa, Oklahoma." Then he grinned at her. "Get used to it," he said.

In the elevator, he pulled her to him. "Mrs. Good Thunder. Mr. and Mrs. Good Thunder and all the little Good Thunders. I like the ring of that. You're going to tame me yet."

"I doubt that," Julie said, and snuggled against his shoulder. "And there's something you haven't told me. Why did my mother open up and tell you so much?"

"Two reasons," he said, his breath warm against her ear. "First, I think she half suspected Rebecca had disappeared on purpose, and she trusted me to keep it to myself if I found out."

She slipped her arms around his waist. "Oh, Jake," she protested. "How could she know that?"

"I don't know. She's sharp, your mother. The longer we talked, the more I felt like we had some weird telepathy. She knew how much I loved you. Somehow, she could tell, and she knew I could see that she understood."

He paused, drew back slightly and grinned down at her. "There's more. She knows I'm going to be the father of the only grandchildren she'll ever have. If her father's line goes on, it's through you and me."

The doors slid open, but Julie couldn't move. She stared up at him, astonished. "Jake!" she said in an almost disbelieving, breathless whisper.

"It's true," he said. "We sat there talking about nothing but Will Albert and Rebecca, but she knew it and I knew it. Our genes are going to mingle."

Julie shook her head in bewilderment. Jake slipped his arm around her shoulders and they stepped from the elevator. "That's too weird for words," she said. "But it's certainly true that, well, Mother isn't exactly like other people."

"When I started thinking about those children after that, they suddenly seemed real, sugar. And I understood why I had to change. A daddy shouldn't specialize in danger. He needs to stick around and see those kids grow up."

They walked down the long hall, looking for room 838. She held his hand, leaned dreamily against his shoulder, saying nothing, only savoring the moment and thinking of those future children. *Mr. and Mrs. Good Thunder. And all the little Good Thunders.*

"Julie," he said, "did Rebecca know about me?"

"Of course she knew about you. I cried on her shoulder like a big baby. She kept saying, 'But, Julie, if you *love* him . . .' And I'd say, 'No, no, no. It'll never work.'"

They came to room 838. Jake took out the key, but he paused a moment. He looked into her eyes. "Do you suppose she knew when she disappeared that you'd turn to me?"

Once again, Julie found tears rising in her eyes. She stared at Jake in wonder. "Oh, Jake. She must have. She'd lost her love, but she wanted me to get mine back. She knew eventually I'd have to turn to you. Maybe she even suspected you'd find the truth and set my mind at ease."

He nodded and smiled. "Maybe she did. She left just enough clues." He laughed softly. "Rebecca," he said. "That little girl with all the imagination and the romantic ideas never got lost, after all."

"No," Julie said, smiling, too. "She didn't."

"If we have a little girl, maybe that's what we ought to name her—Rebecca. Rebecca Lynn."

Jake unlocked the door, then swept her up into his arms and kissed her. "I'd better practice," he said, "so I'll be sure to get this right."

He kissed her again and carried her over the threshold.